PRAISE FOR VINCENT ZANDRI

"Sensational...masterful...brilliant."

—New York Post

"My fear level rose with this Zandri novel like it hasn't done before. Wondering what the killer had in store for Jude and seeing the ending, well, this is one book that will be with me for a long time to come!"

—Reviews by Molly

"I very highly recommend this book...It's a great crime drama that is full of action and intense suspense, along with some great twists...Vincent Zandri has become a huge name and just keeps pouring out one best seller after another."

—*Life in Review*

"(The Innocent) is a thriller that has depth and substance, wickedness and compassion."

—*The Times-Union* (Albany)

"I also sat on the edge of my seat reading about Jude trying to stay alive when he was thrown into one of those games...Add to that having to disarm a bomb for good measure!"

—Telly Says

"The action never wanes."

—*Fort Lauderdale Sun-Sentinal*

"Gritty, fast-paced, lyrical and haunting."

—Harlan Coben, bestselling author of *Six Years*

"Tough, stylish, heartbreaking."

—Don Winslow, bestselling author of *Savages*

CHASE BAKER
AND THE
LINCOLN CURSE

(A Chase Baker Thriller #4)

VINCENT ZANDRI

"The truth is I have never loved Henry more than I have this last month. I have wanted to wail with pity over him... He mutters more than ever of our hours in the box at Ford's, forcing me to think of them, too."

—*Clara Harris Rathbone speaking of her husband, Henry Rathbone, on the eve of their murder/suicide, December 23, 1893.*

What follows is inspired by true events.

PROLOGUE

Good Friday, April 14, 1865
Ford's Theater
Washington, DC
10:19PM

THE PRESIDENT HAS BEEN SHOT.

Triggered at point-blank range by John Wilkes Booth, a twenty-six-year-old fanatic Confederate sympathizer and stage actor, the bullet has managed to crack President Lincoln's skull open like an egg. More specifically, the solid lead ball has penetrated the bone behind the left earlobe and lodged itself just above his right eye, nearly exiting the forehead. Despite frantic attempts by a physician (whom, it should be noted, is attending the evening performance of Our American Cousin at the invitation of the White House) to remove the bullet with his fingers, the projectile is lodged too deep inside the brainpan. He does, however, manage to remove some of the thicker blood clots, a process which is believed to help protect the President's circulatory system from collapsing entirely.

When the decision is made to move the President from the box down the narrow staircase to the lobby, the two Union soldiers and one heavyset grocer who are chosen for the task, move swiftly. The President's head is bleeding a profuse amount of dark red, nearly black arterial blood. Knowing a bumpy carriage ride back to the White House will finish the President off for good, the men transport him instead across the street to the three-story Peterson house. There, the deadweight body is laid out diagonally across a bed far too small for its long legs, arms, and torso.

By the President's side is the short, stout, black-haired Mary Lincoln, who holds his lifeless hand tightly while a team of three doctor's attempt in vain to resuscitate him, despite a fading pulse. Seated beside Mary, embracing her, is one of the two people who occupied the Presidential Box during the stage performance—the attractive, slightly built woman's name is Clara Harris. She and her fiancé, Union Major Henry Rathbone, were only too happy to attend the play after General Grant and his wife declined.

Near death himself, the tall, mustached Henry Rathbone is attended to by a fourth doctor who tries to stem the flow of blood that comes from a bone-deep gash extending from elbow to shoulder. The wound was received when Rathbone attempted to apprehend Booth after the Southern sympathizer made the fatal shot with a .44 caliber Derringer. If Henry had been able to make the jump on the killer just a split second earlier, he might have prevented Lincoln's murder. But it was not to be.

As Mary Lincoln wails in agony for God to spare her husband's life, she turns to the petite, and far younger, Clara, resting her sobbing head in the woman's lap.

"Your dress," Mary cries, "it's covered in my husband's blood."

Clara reaches out with her small, almost fragile hand, touches the blood-soaked fabric. She slowly turns to view her fiancé, who sits close by in a chair, wrestling both consciousness and an ever growing guilt over not having prevented the President's assassination.

"That's Henry's blood, too," Clara whispers, turning back to the distraught First Lady. "Henry tried to stop the President's killer. Do you understand, Mrs. Lincoln?"

Sitting up slowly, Mary gazes upon Henry, locking eyes with the distressed young man.

"You did your best, Major," she says, her eyes cold and distant. "I understand you did...your best."

Just then, a gasp, and a final breath exhaled.

Mary turns back to her husband, shoots up from her chair.

"He's dead!" she wails. "My husband is dead!"

1

Albany Rural Cemetery
Albany, NY
Present Day

IT'S TRUE WHAT THEY SAY. YOU CAN'T GO HOME AGAIN.
Not as anything other than a visitor and certainly not
for very long. Which is why I almost never come back to
this city of barely one hundred thousand inhabitants.

Home being Albany. A city where nothing much
ever happens and nothing much ever changes. It's as if
Father Time crossed it off his checklist and passed it by
entirely.

But, sometimes you just can't avoid having to scrape
together the money for a train ticket that will take you
along the Hudson River line north to the place where
you grew up and, in the process, experienced all your

4

firsts—both good and bad. First communion. First ass kicking in the school yard. First kicking of ass in the school yard. First Pop Warner football game. First girlfriend. First kiss. First base. First time on second. First Time on third. First time you slide into home plate, regardless of how sloppy and awkward the process.

...*Thanks, for the memories...*

It's also the place you snatched your first real job. At least, that's how it happened in my case when I went to work for the old man at the ripe old age of twelve. Now that I think about it, my old man wasn't all that old at the time. He was maybe ten years younger than I am now when I went to work excavating and sandhogging for the Tommy Baker Excavating company. It was a job that had been waiting for me since birth and, in many ways, a job that I was expected to perform, regardless of the fact that one day becoming a writer and an explorer, just like Jack London, had become my dream even as a pre-teen.

But then, according to my old man, dreams were for silly people. What mattered was the earth you could hold in your hand and scoop up with a mechanized bucket. The earth was as real as something could possibly get. Like Dad always said, "From dirt we came and to dirt we will return."

Digging in the dirt also paid well. Very well, in fact. Something my dad always tried to impress upon me as my adolescence turned into young adulthood, and adulthood shifted towards middle age. "Being a writer and an explorer and even a private detective are all noble occupations indeed, son," he said to me not long before he died. "But being noble does not pay the bills. You should know that by now."

If only Dad could take a quick look at my less than stellar bank account these days, he'd force a shovel in my hand and bark, "Now get to work!"

But, back in the days when I had my whole life ahead of me, I quickly came to realize that being a digger with Dad's company didn't mean I had to put all of my dreams on hold. In fact, sandhogging afforded me some significant exploration experience, especially when Dad was hired by some university or college to excavate archeological sites that took us all the way around the world to Egypt or Peru or even China. We weren't by any means the most important men on an archeological dig. If anything, we were considered—by the more educated, doctoral treasure hunters—to be a bit of an unwashed and untamed nuisance.

But let me tell you, there's no better thrill in the world than feeling the tooth of a backhoe bucket touching upon a stone sarcophagus. A gentle, yet powerful, sensation that travels from the ancient stone into the empty bucket, up the backhoe arm, into the cab, through the controls, and straight into flesh and bone. Dad knew this feeling all too well, which is why he chose to work with the schools on their digs in place of more lucrative jobs like digging foundations for commercial buildings all over the city. Dad was no stranger to his own noble pursuits now and then, too.

But, despite the golden opportunity of his handing me the keys to his business one day, I think Dad knew I wouldn't be able to call Albany home for too long, even if we did spend considerable time away from it on our various adventures. The world was a big place, to be sure. My dreams were even bigger. And Albany was way too small and, well, way too small-minded for my tastes.

Which is why I took off when I had the chance, venturing off to lands unknown, supporting myself any way I could. Sure, Dad was disappointed (and on occasion worried), but I also like to think he was proud of me in his own way. What father doesn't want his son to make it on his own, no matter the difficulties and the dangers? That didn't prevent him from sending me a much-needed check now and again. A practice he lovingly maintained even after I turned the corner on forty.

Now, I've come back home for one last meeting with dad.

How is it possible to meet with someone who's been dead for almost six years? Dad's about to be exhumed and reinterred which, in plain language, means his casket is going to be dug up, opened, and whatever's left of his corpse transferred to another, newer casket which will be laid to rest in a vacant piece of cemetery property located elsewhere. Why? So that the land his present grave occupies can be utilized for a new town road.

Sorry Pop, but that's progress for you...

In honor of Dad and the many cash favors he did for me over the years, I volunteered my services for excavating his grave, which involved an official application to the cemetery that would require signatures from both the local Albany Police Department and the Albany Hall of Records. Once my services were approved, the cemetery allowed me use of their backhoe, which turns out to be an old, somewhat rusted CAT that probably rolled off the assembly line while I was doing bong hits in my Providence College dorm room.

After issuing a smile and a nod to both the County Coroner and the head of cemetery maintenance, who've both shown up for the event, I climb into the cab and sit myself down in a black pleather seat held together with matching black electrical tape. Turning the seat around so that it faces the bucket, I place my hands on the controls. The round, heavy-duty plastic handles attached to the floor-mounted sticks feel like an old friend. So does the smell of gasoline and oil when I toe tap the gas, sending a burst of power into the engine.

Maybe you never forget how to ride a bike, but the same can be said of running a backhoe, especially when you were trained by your old man back when you were twelve and could barely reach the pedals. As I feel the vibration of the machine, I send the sharp metal teeth into the green, grass-covered soil, and scoop out the first full yard of Dad's own earth, depositing it off to the side. I continue the process until I feel that familiar tap of the metal tooth on hard concrete, and I know I'm home. I'm knocking on the concrete encasement that houses Dad's casket.

Slipping out of the cab, I instruct the cemetery workers to apply the chain to the backhoe and the reinforced concrete casement cover.

"Let's pull my dad out of the ground," I say. "And be careful not to wake him."

Half an hour later, my dad's surprisingly water damaged casket is set off to the side of his now open grave and the gravestone that watches over it. The cemetery keeper is standing by, as is the coroner who must be present at all exhumations. While the workers have no choice but to use a pry bar to open a lid sealed shut due to rust, I feel my heart beating in my throat. I mean, I know my dad's a dead guy, but why do I feel like I'm the prodigal son? Why do I feel like once the casket lid opens, my dad's gonna sit up straight, look me in the eye, and say, "Chase, it's about time you grew up, came home, and took over the excavation business."

My mouth goes dry. My feet feel like they aren't planted on solid ground but, instead, are levitating a foot above the earth. A click reverberates across the tree-covered, rolling, green cemetery plain. The lid's pried open. Then, acting in unison, the two workers lift the heavy cover. For a brief moment, they lock eyes on the body that's inside and then, stepping back and away from the box, shoot me a look indicating that it's my turn.

I step forward and, with my heart pulsing up against my sternum, peer into the casket.

2

TO SAY MY DAD LOOKS PRETTY GOOD FOR A GUY WHO'S been dead going on six years is an exaggeration. I mean, what should a man dead that long look like anyway? But I can say this, he doesn't look all that bad. Standing before the open casket, I'm reminded of a story my grandfather once told me about the last person left alive to have born witness to the body of President Abraham Lincoln. The man, who was a young boy in the early 1920s at the time, had accompanied his father to Lincoln's grave in Washington, DC which was being exhumed in order to reinter the body into a tomb that would be buried entirely in concrete. In other words, a tomb so sound and incorruptible it would be safe even from the most passionate grave robber.

Story goes that while a handful of workers opened up Lincoln's casket, the boy looked on in awe. He was also more than a little bit frightened. But when the boy caught sight of the tall, bearded man dressed in the black suit of the mid-1800s, the rose he'd been buried with still pinned to his lapel, he knew precisely who he was looking at.

Abe Lincoln.

What shocked the boy most about the body was not the smell, which was both sweet and stale, but the President's skin which had turned entirely black. As if in death, God had turned Lincoln into the very species of man he fought so hard to liberate and, in turn, took a bullet to the head for his efforts.

The same can be said of my dad.

In the six years since he'd first been buried, his skin has turned a rich, brown-black. It's also shrunk, covering his bony skull like a mask more than an actual face. Aside from the occasional moth-like hole, his suit looks just as fresh as it did the day we laid him to rest. And, just like Lincoln, his boutonniere is still pinned to his lapel, even if it has grayed and dried over time.

Reaching into the casket, I place my hand on top of his now bone-thin hands which are resting on a concave stomach.

"Hi, Dad," I say. "We're gonna get you some new digs today. Better joint, with a better view. A nice new casket and nice new neighbors, too. You're gonna love it."

I look into his eyes, which are closed and flat, and I imagine his response.

"Just hurry it up, Kid. It's cold up here."

Wiping damp eyes with the backs of my hands, I turn away from the casket.

"You guys can do the rest," I say, stepping past the coroner and the cemetery keeper, my eyes focused on the pickup truck rental parked on the near shoulder of the inner cemetery road. I don't cover more than twenty feet before the cop cruiser pulls up and a man steps out.

"You Chase Baker?" he says.

"Depends on who's asking."

"The APD is asking. And trust me when we say we don't like to repeat ourselves."

3

HE'S A TALL GUY. TALLER THAN ME ANYWAY. OLDER TOO, but in pretty good shape. The old-fashioned trenchcoat he's wearing makes him look like a character from an old Sam Fuller detective movie. *The Naked Kiss* maybe. Or *Pickup on South Street*. Pulp films aired on the Saturday CBS Late Night Movie back when I was a kid. Movies the old man forbade me to watch on the portable black and white set up in my room, but that I watched anyway, punishment be damned. Chase the ballsy.

His full head of hair is white and cut like a jar-headed Marine and if I have to guess, I'd say he's no stranger to the local road racing circuit. I peg him for the type of police officer who wouldn't know what the hell to do with himself if he were to retire, since it's rare to find one still on the job at his age. In my experience anyway.

"My name is Nick Miller," he says. "Homicide Detective Nick Miller, you want the full formal boat." Holding out his hand. "Sorry to disturb you on such a, what shall I call it, solemn occasion."

I take the extended hand in mind, squeeze it hard to show him that I'm tough and dangerous even if my .45 isn't stored against my ribs like it usually is.

"Chase," I say. "Chase Baker. But then, you probably already know that."

He squints blue eyes, his point of view shifting from me to Dad's still open casket back to me again.

"Gotta say," he says, raising his hand, tossing the coroner a quick but polite wave, "I've witnessed more than my fair share of exhumations over the course of my career, especially when a witness or a defendant wasn't entirely convinced that a perp was safely buried six feet under. But I've never seen a family member actually get involved in the excavation process. I was surprised when I saw your name on the application."

"It's in our bones," I say. "I used to be a digger and a sandhog." Crossing my arms. "Thought you said you were a homicide detective. How'd you see my name on the application in the first place?"

He cocks his head. "We're pathologically understaffed at the APD, meaning we all pitch in where we can, whether we like it or not. Plus, cops can't keep their mouth shut. When a not so unknown guy like you comes back into town with the specific intent to dig up his dad, word gets around pretty fast."

Me, relaxing my arms. "SmAlbany."

"Exactly," he says. "You haven't forgotten. So what exactly is a Sandhog?"

"We work archeological sites. Dig up ancient artifacts. Stuff like that."

"Like Indiana Jones." He winks.

"Not really, but if that helps you understand what we do then yes, like Indy. Now, what can I do for you, Detective? I'd like to get back to New York. I'm working on a new novel and God knows I need the advance check something awful."

"Word on the street is that you're a bit of a Renaissance man, Mr. Baker," he says. "Digger like his father before him, treasure hunter, published novelist, and even a private detective from time to time. It's the last of these talents I'm interested in right now."

I take a step forward, dig my truck keys from out of the pocket on my worn bush jacket, or what my spunky ten-year-old daughter refers to as "Dad's silly jungle jacket."

"I don't work up here, Detective," I say, walking towards my truck. "I'm only here to see that my dad gets his new home and then I'm on my way."

"I just told you we're understaffed and could use a seasoned private dick to pick up the slack. The job also comes with a pretty decent payout. Three hundred per day plus expenses."

The little hairs on the back of my neck prick up. But not enough to keep me from my writing desk. After all, a published book is the financial gift that keeps on giving, year after year after year.

I keep on walking.

"Abraham Lincoln," he says. "The job involves digging up brand new dirt on President Abraham Lincoln."

The keys gripped in my hand, I stop. Turn.

"Lincoln," I say. "As in the Abe shot-in-the-back-of-the-head-by-John-Wilkes-Booth-up-in-that-creepy-Ford's-Theater-Box Lincoln."

"The Abraham Lincoln assassination," he nods. "Were you aware there's a direct archeological link between Lincoln's murder on April 14, 1865 and to your humble hometown of Albany, New York? The hamlet of Loudonville right up the road here to be exact?" He raises his right hand, points his thumb over his shoulder in the direction he's referring to.

I shake my head, but I sense he knows exactly how to bait a history hunter like me. Then, once snagged, how to reel me in without breaking the fishing line. Cash payoff or no cash payoff.

"Tell you what," he says, "why don't we take a quick ride? If you don't like what I'm showing you, or it doesn't get a rise out of you, or the money's not worth it, then no harm done. Have a nice trip back down south or across the pond or both and good luck on the new novel. Fair enough?"

I just want to get out of Albany, get back to work, now that I've seen Dad for what will surely be the last time. But Abraham Lincoln. His assassination. Some sort of archeological connection to my hometown. How can I not be interested? The blood racing through my veins should be proof enough of that.

"Okay, Detective, I'm sufficiently hooked."

His face lights up as he opens the back door on his cruiser, motions his hand to direct me that way.

"Get in," he says.

Exhaling a breath, I get in the car. He shuts the door behind me, slips into the front shotgun seat while the uniformed cop behind the wheel pulls out.

"We gonna stop for donuts on the way?" I say.

"Very funny," Miller says. "Gotta love private dicks. Even part-time ones like yourself."

"Sorry," I say, as we drive through the cemetery gates, "couldn't resist." Chase the comedian.

4

WE DRIVE DOWN A BUSY SUBURBAN ROAD IN A WESTERLY direction for maybe a mile until we come to the intersection of the main north/south street connecting the city of Albany with the Northern suburbs. The official state designation of the byway is Route 9 or Loudon Road. But, the square blue placard installed on the roadside by the Albany Historical Society claims its original name to be the "Kings Highway" after King George whose army of Redcoats used it as a supply route between Albany and Fort William Henry fifty-plus miles to the North on the aptly named Lake George. Or so I quickly read through the backseat window while stopped at the traffic signal.

The hamlet of Loudonville was also a popular stopover for weary travelers looking for a hot meal and a warm bed for the night—historical information about my hometown that I am not entirely unfamiliar with, but never took a special interest in before. Now I know it has something to do with Abe Lincoln's murder, though.

We proceed south in the direction of the city along a stretch of roadway that I'm perfectly acquainted with since it's where all the rich people live. Lining both sides of the King's Road are mega-houses built before the war—World War II that is—set on plots of land large enough to support small neighborhoods. After about a mile, the driver hooks a right onto Cherry Tree Road and slowly makes the drive up a steady incline, coming to a stop outside the second house on the left-hand side.

It's an old white colonial with black shutters built prior to the war all right...the Civil War. It's been added onto over the decades so that what must have started out as a simple two-story cottage, has now become a large home that lacks any semblance of symmetry with its attached rooms and bedrooms. The place looks more like an inn or bed-and-breakfast you might stop at for the night in rural Vermont than a residence for a single family.

The place is also shuttered.

Yellow ribbon containing block letters that read KEEP OUT. CRIME SCENE. surrounds the lawn like a makeshift fence. Some of the same yellow ribbon covers a front door which also sports a piece of thick plywood screwed over the opening.

We sit and stare at the house for a minute, as if waiting for it to do something like wink at us, for instance.

"Crime scene," I say after a time. "I'll bite. What happened here that makes it a crime scene? And why's it boarded up like that?"

Miller sets his elbow on the seatback, peers at me over his shoulder.

"It's not just a crime scene, like the tape says. It's also considered hallowed ground by some. You might even say the story of Lincoln's assassination doesn't end in DC, but right here instead."

"I'm not following."

"You ever heard of Clara Harris and Major Henry Rathbone, Baker?"

I rack my brain for a connection, but the names are unfamiliar.

"Here's an irony for you considering my chosen career path: I got a C in American History, Detective."

"Well, I'm told William Faulkner flunked freshman English at Mississippi U. And even if you got an A in history, I'm still not sure you would've heard of them. They've become a sort of footnote in the annals of one of the country's most notorious murders."

Just then a car comes up on our right side, pulls over in front of the cruiser, parks. It's a black BMW. A man gets out. He's big and portly, his hair black and wavy, but so long in the back it hangs off his shoulders. He's sporting a thick black handlebar mustache, and he's wearing a brown ascot to go with his brown wool jacket.

"Who's that?" I ask. "The ghost from another century past?"

"Our resident Lincoln historian," Miller says, gesturing with his hand for the heavyset, mustached man to hop into the cruiser. "This guy most definitely got an A in American history. Trust me on that."

The back door opens and the man gets in, sitting himself down heavily.

"Mr. Chase Baker, please meet Albany State University Professor of History and Civil War Reenactment aficionado, Theodore Balkis. Ted Balkis, please meet Chase Baker."

19

The professor holds out his hand. I grab it and shake. It's thick and puffy. Feels like a cold, wet fish. A blowfish maybe. I release the hand, wipe the perspiration on my pant leg discreetly.

"You're no stranger to archeological digs, so I hear?" Balkis says, reaching into his jacket pocket, pulling out a kerchief to wipe beaded sweat from his brow. The inflection in his voice is sort of uppity. Snobbish. Like a wealthy Long Island lock-jawed housewife speaking down to you. It's also a bit on the effeminate side, also just like a Long Island housewife.

I shoot a glance at Miller.

"Looks like more than a few people knew I was making the trip up here," I say.

"Told you," he says. "We really need your help and we're willing to fork out some of Albany's hard-earned tax dollars in exchange for it."

Eyes back on Balkis.

"I've been on my share of digs," I say. "Mostly I write. On occasion, I'm a private detective, among other things. Money's always tight these days and self-employment taxes are a bitch."

"A man with many hats. How I envy you the freedom to be whatever you want to be, taxes be damned. Have I read anything you've written?"

I let the question go ignored, because if he's gotta ask...

Miller breaks in, "As you know, Ted, I brought Mr. Baker here to see if he could help with our little problem here at the Clara Harris Rathbone house. I thought you might first fill him in on the history of the joint."

Balkis smiles. "I'd be happy to fill him in on the history of the uhhh...*joint*...as you so aptly put it, Detective." Then, he looks at me, with big dark eyes. "But it all begins with April 14, 1865. So what do you know about the Lincoln assassination mystery, Mr. Baker?"

I shrug my shoulders like I'm back in high school history class thinking about girls and working on that C.

"What mystery?" I say. "Wasn't the mystery of who shot Lincoln and why solved when John Wilkes Booth was cornered and killed?"

"Precisely," Balkis says. "But few people know about the man who nearly prevented the assassination from happening along with the true story of what happened to the murder weapons. You see, Mr. Baker, it all begins with a young couple who were invited to share the Presidential Box with the Lincolns on the night of the assassination. One, Union Major Henry Rathbone and his fiancée, Clara Harris."

While we sit in the car staring out at the silent house, Balkis goes on to tell a tragic story about two young, seemingly normal people, caught up in some extraordinary historical circumstances when the box they occupied in Ford's Theater was invaded by John Wilkes Booth—the tall, handsome, fiercely Southern Confederate actor who put the barrel of a Derringer to Lincoln's head and pulled the trigger, changing the course of American—if not world—history forever.

"You see, Mr. Baker," the professor goes on, "the moment Booth burst into the box, Henry Rathbone tried to save his President by leaping towards the killer's gun. My guess is he would have gladly taken the bullet himself. But he was just too far away and Booth was able to complete his grisly deed.

"However, that didn't stop Henry from apprehending the killer. But Booth was packing a fighting knife with an eight-inch blade, and he managed to cut Henry's arm so badly he nearly bled out on the spot."

"So what's this house got to do with what you're telling me?"

"Although Clara and Henry settled in Washington, DC after they were married, this home is where they came to live during the hot summer months since it was close to Clara's father who worked in the New York State Senate. Among the personal articles they brought with them into the marriage and into this house were the white dress that Clara wore on that fateful night...a dress that was stained with both her husband's blood and the blood from the President. They also brought with them the Derringer that killed Lincoln and the fighting knife that cut Henry's arm."

My pulse picks up. I grew up in this community, not far from here. If what he's saying is gospel,

I had no idea what lie right under my nose—the relics and the history.

"Shouldn't that stuff have immediately gone to a museum?" I say.

"One would think so," Balkis says. "But after the assassination trial and the executions that followed, Henry Rathbone began to obsess with Lincoln's murder. He began to plague himself with the question: *What if I'd just been a little bit quicker?* Well, sir, perhaps if he had been just a little bit quicker, he might have indeed saved the President's life."

It strikes me as odd that Professor Balkis, who is clearly a Yankee, sometimes takes on a fake southern accent. But then, he's clearly got a flair for the dramatic, at least, judging from the way he dresses and styles himself. I can only wonder which side he chooses during the civil war reenactments.

"What happened to Henry and Clara?"

"They had three kids—two boys and a girl. They tried raising them as responsible parents, but the assassination always hung over them like a beating, bleeding heart. And as time went on, their mental capacities, especially Henry's, began to disintegrate. Clara became convinced that Lincoln occupied her house, cursing the place forever. Meanwhile, Henry also believed that Lincoln was visiting him at the house and that Lincoln wasn't happy with him. You see, the President blamed the Major for not saving him from Booth's bullet."

Balkis sets his beefy sweaty hand on my thigh sufficiently creeping me out.

"What happened after that?" I say, shaking the hand off.

"Legend has it that Rathbone began to drink heavily. His behavior became erratic. The US Army had no choice but to retire him as a Colonel. He scared the children with his tirades and rants. He shouted out the name of Lincoln in his sleep. He shouted out the name of Booth. Once, he even attacked Clara in the middle of the night while they lie together in bed, thinking she was the Booth of his dreams."

Balkis' eyes grow wider with each word spoken, each bit of information revealed. Like a world-class orator gracing the stage.

"It all became worse," he goes on, his voice now assuming a nefarious, low-key tone. "On the anniversary of Lincoln's assassination, reporters would come from far away and beg to speak with the two people, besides Mary Lincoln, who last saw the President alive. Always the question of why Henry didn't do more would arise, driving him even madder. In a word, life had become unbearable with the tremendous burden of Lincoln's assassination weighing so heavily on his shoulders.

"Then, as the story goes, Christmas of 1893 while they were living at the summer house for the holidays,

Henry went into a rage, believing not only that Clara was having an affair, but that she was doing so out of shame for his having failed to save the President. Henry went upstairs to his bedroom. There he found the Derringer and the fighting knife in his top dresser drawer where it was stored along with Clara's blood-stained dress."

The portly professor is now making like a pistol with one hand and a fist with the other as if gripping a knife.

"Loading the pistol and pocketing the knife, he headed back downstairs where, in front of the children and their Christmas tree, he shot his wife in the back of her head. Dropping the pistol, he pulled out his knife and proceeded to stab himself in the stomach multiple times. Some say he survived and was institutionalized, but many believe he died that night and that it took him twelve agonizing hours to die. The exact amount of hours it took Lincoln to die, as if Rathbone had made a contract with God for it to happen that way. However..." His voice trails off.

"However what?" I say.

"No one has ever confirmed the Henry Rathbone/Clara Harris murder/suicide story. No police reports were ever filed, and nothing exists in the Hall of Records other than a statement about their being buried in the Albany Rural Cemetery in a family plot purchased years earlier."

"You ask a homicide dick like me," Miller interjects, "It's a made up bedtime story...that the truth behind their deaths isn't nearly as dramatic."

The car goes silent again while once more I stare through the glass at the house. Regardless of the truth, it's hard to believe such a peaceful, if not quaint, cottage-looking residence could have sheltered such a dysfunctional family. A historical dysfunctional family.

CHASE BAKER AND THE LINCOLN CURSE

"It's been said that as soon as Henry and Clara were buried, Henry Riggs Rathbone Jr. handed over the Derringer and the knife to the authorities who, in turn, delivered them to the Ford's Theater Museum. As for the dress, however, he wanted to retain it, as if there was a special power that went with it. A curse even. In the ensuing years, he stored in the back of Clara's closet, a solid brick wall constructed before it, to hide it away forever.

"But in 1910, Junior is purported to have broken through the brick wall in Clara's bedroom. Convinced the dress had haunted his family long enough, he retrieved the bloody dress and burned it, thus destroying the curse. But to this day, like so many other aspects of the legend, no evidence of the burned remnants have ever been confirmed, leaving some to speculate that the dress still exists. There are also rumors that the Derringer and fighting knife housed in the Ford's Theater Museum in Washington are fakes, indicating that Junior never did relinquish the true artifacts after the death of his parents...that the real McCoys are still out there somewhere waiting to be discovered. Perhaps they were both wrapped in Clara's bloody dress. Now, wouldn't that be the find of the century, Mr. Baker?"

He puts his hand on my leg again. I shake it away *again*.

"This all sounds like folklore, if you ask me," I say.

Balkis gives Miller a look like they're communicating without speaking.

"So what do you want with me?" I go on. "Why am I here and not back in New York City, Detective Miller?"

He says, "The couple who lived in this house up until a few weeks ago, have gone missing. Been missing for almost a week now."

"So isn't it your job to find them? You or the FBI?"

"Sure it is, Baker," he says. "It's just that we've reached a bit of a brick wall, if you'll pardon the pun, and we just don't have the personnel or the resources right now to break it down. I'm hesitant to involve the Feds at this stage of the game."

"Sorry, Detective. Still not sure how I can help."

"I was hoping you might give the case a try. See what you can come up with. Like I said, I can do three hundred per day plus expenses. I might even toss in some donuts."

"Really?" I say. "Dunkin Donuts. Not store bought. I'm partial to blueberry cakes."

"Absolutely, Chase. Dunkin Donut blueberry cakes. You sure drive a hard bargain."

"I didn't go into business with my dad, but some of his smarts wore off on me." Then, "My guess is the couple who lived here left the country. That is, they didn't want to be found. Were they wanted for something in particular?"

"I'm not sure they're capable of leaving the country much less the city, Baker," he says. "And I'm not entirely sure they're wanted for anything. Don't let the crime scene tape fool you. That's why I haven't called the Feds in."

"Can you be any more cryptic, Miller?"

He shoots the professor another look.

"I'm gonna tell him, Ted," he says. "I'm gonna spill the damn beans."

"Can't hurt," Ted says.

5

MILLER'S EYES BACK ON ME.

"The couple who've lived here for nearly sixty years were the first people to occupy the place since Henry, Jr. They recently entered into a sale of the historic home to Albany State University—"

"—which is where I come in."

"Yes, which is where Ted comes in."

"Excuse me, Detective. But that would be Dr. Balkis if you don't mind." He says it using his faux Southern accent again.

Miller goes stone-faced. "Yes, that would be Herr Dr. Balkis." He says Balkis, like Ball Kiss. It gets a snicker out of the driver. "In any case, Baker, the present owners, a Mr. and Mrs. Bill Girvin, are pushing ninety. Eccentric couple in that they lived in the house exactly as Clara Harris and Henry Rathbone and their family would have lived in it in the mid-eighteen hundreds. No running water, no electricity. Fires to heat the place...You get my drift. At one time, back in the forties and fifties, they even used a horse and buggy to get around town. He can barely walk, and his wife is said to be stricken with Alzheimer's. So I'm not entirely sure they're capable of boarding a plane to Europe much less making it out the front door without collapsing onto the front lawn."

"Maybe they were kidnaped," I say.

Miller nods.

"Excellent," he says. "Except for one thing, there's no sign of a break-in. No sign of a struggle. No notes passed on to us asking for a ransom from Girvin's estate which is sizable. More than sizeable, his inheritance money older than Lincoln himself. No strange prints anywhere in the house."

"What's forensics have to say?"

"They did their best to check the joint out. But it's so old and who knows the origins of the oddball prints they picked up."

"So how do you know something criminal went down here?"

"What we did find is blood. Small, but still significant traces up inside the bedroom where Clara hid the white dress."

"Blood," I repeat. "Who's blood?"

"Blood from both Girvins," Miller says. "Or so the lab reports confirm. We also found a .44 caliber pocket cannon on the bed, beside a fighting knife, the blade painted red with both Girvin's DNA."

6

"So let me get this straight," I say after a beat.
"The owners of this home are missing. They're almost as old as Lincoln himself, and they disappeared without a trace after a Derringer and a fighting knife just like the ones used in the Lincoln assassination are discovered up in Clara's old bedroom."

"The pistol had been discharged, by the way," Miller adds. "We've taken both items into custody, bagged and tagged them as evidence. They're not the original pieces that killed Lincoln and cut Rathbone, but some skillfully forged knockoffs. Or so I'm told."

Balkis nods.

"What the hell happened here?" I ask.

"Something violent causing blood to be spilled. That's all I can conclude until I locate the Girvins, dead or alive."

"Are you asking me to find the Girvins or find the dress?"

"You're an expert in finding missing people, especially when they're connected to some kind of antiquity or relic or treasure."

"You want me to find a pair of old people who are likely to be dead. You should dredge the river, Detective Miller."

"Maybe," he says.

"What if the Lincoln curse somehow got to Girvin? Maybe he, too, lost his mind and tried to mimic Rathbone and Clara and their murder-suicide?"

"Always a possibility," Miller says. "But people tend not to run very far after a murder-suicide. Again, I need to find them in order to prove anything."

"Uh, I'm not saying the curse is anything but legend, but wouldn't it have died along with the burned dress?"

Balkis clears his throat.

"Or perhaps," he says, "Clara's white dress wasn't burned in the first place, and still resides in the house somewhere in some secret chamber or ante-chamber just waiting to be found. That would mean for certain the curse still exists. Who knows what might be discovered inside that house if only the police would let us back inside."

"Listen, Professor," Miller, barks, "If I told you once, I told you a thousand times, no one goes into that house until this investigation is finished, you got me?"

Balkis turns to me.

"Unfortunately, the good detective here feels the need to treat me like a little child. He won't allow me access to the house all on my own. Calls it a breach of forensic procedural protocol or some such legalese nonsense."

"You and the university will have your shot, Professor, when all this is over," Miller adds.

"Sure," Balkis says, opening the door. "When an entire team of university scholars and their camera crews descend upon the place. No, thank you. I prefer to work on my own."

He gets out, slams the door shut, wobbles over to his car, gets in. Firing up the engine, he makes an abrupt three-point turn and heads in the opposite direction, back towards the Kings Highway, not bothering to give us a second look.

"He's uptight, that one," I say. "A little weird, too."

"You have no idea," Miller says. Then, "So, will you give the job some thought?"

"You really think I'll be able to do a better job of finding the old couple than you and your staff will?" I ask.

"Can't hurt to try."

I take another look at the house. At the boarded up door.

"Can I get into the joint?"

Miller reaches into his pocket, comes out with a set of keys, tosses them to me.

"Those are for you and you *only*. Balkis manages to get inside, there's no telling what he'll pocket. Guy knows his history, but he's a bit off kilter, you ask me." He extends his index finger, makes a twirling motion with it around his temple. "Key works on the back door off the kitchen. Remember, Balkis finds out you have a set and he doesn't, he'll go all ballistic on me like a three-year-old denied a lollipop."

"Why even bother to work with the guy?"

"Like I said. He knows too much."

"About the Girvin's?"

"No. About Lincoln and that creepy house's history.

In his mind, he's not reenacting the Civil War. He is *in* the Civil War."

I smile. "Don't tell me you believe in curses, ghosts, and a whole lot of hocus pocus campfire stories, Detective Miller?"

He cocks his head, grins like he's on the fence about believing versus not believing.

"Who really knows what spirits lurk behind those old walls," he whispers, biting down on his lip.

The way he says it makes the fine hairs on the back of my neck stand up. "Can you take me back to my truck?"

Miller turns back to the front.

"Daylight's wasting," he says, like John Wayne.

We drive.

7

I SIT IN THE PICKUP WATCHING THE CEMETERY CREW LOAD Dad onto a casket truck flatbed with the help of a chain and winch. Sure, he can't feel anything anymore. Scratch that...What I mean is, it's possible if not entirely probable, that he ceases to exist in any form imaginable. That is, if you don't believe in a soul being an entirely separate energy source from blood, flesh, and bone.

Maybe you believe in ghosts. Or maybe you don't. But as I sit here, watching the old, water-stained coffin (so much for supposedly waterproof concrete coffin chambers) now making its way from the open grave to its new home, I can't help believe that somehow my dad is, at present, watching my every move, watching his own physical body...what's left of it...being transported to yet another resting place. Maybe, like I discovered not too long ago while searching for an Indian God Boy with six arms, it's possible the dead don't sleep the sleep of the dead after all. It's possible they are instead reborn into something else entirely, be it a kind of living spirit or even another human being.

Maybe the same can be said of Abraham Lincoln and the curse that surrounds him. Did he, in fact, haunt Henry Rathbone to the point of madness? To the point of homicide? To the point of suicide? Or was Henry Rathbone just a nutcase, plain and simple?

What about the Girvins? What drives a seemingly normal man to attack his wife and himself, if that is indeed what happened upstairs in their old home? Maybe the ghost of Henry Rathbone made him do it? Maybe the ghost of Lincoln made him do it, or all of the above? Or, maybe I'm letting my imagination get to me.

Did I really believe in curses? Maybe the old coot and the wife simply walked away from the house in a haze of derangement exacerbated by old age and senility.

It's been known to happen from time to time, especially at homes for the elderly. An old woman is found on the street corner, bags in hand, her face awkwardly made up with lipstick and rouge, while still dressed in her pajamas. "I'm moving back home," she'll inevitably announce when the white coats finally get hold of her.

Or maybe an old couple manages to book tickets on a Greyhound Bus to Florida. Once there, they check into a cheap seaside motel and swallow cyanide capsules. Who knows what the brain is capable of once it reaches a certain age? Once it begins to be shadowed by its own death every minute of every day.

But how did that Lincoln assassination Derringer knockoff get inside the bedroom? How did that fighting knife get up there? If the knife was covered in old man and old lady Girvin's blood, then surely they are dead by now. But where do they rest?

That's the question Miller is paying me to find out, isn't it?

First things first.

If indeed the Girvin's are dead, then what's to prevent me from making a search for Clara Harris' bloodied white dress? After all, it's quite possible that the story of her son burning it 1910 is a fabrication, and I have a key to the joint.

Chase the inquisitive...Chase the explorer.

I start the truck, throw her into drive.

"Take care, Dad," I say, tossing one more glance at the casket truck.

"Take care of yourself, Son," I hear him say. "Thanks for stopping by and digging me up. The personal touch means a lot. And for God's sakes, watch your back with this Clara-Harris-bloody-dress-Lincoln-curse thing. I know the money's good and a gig is a gig, but remember, not everything is what it seems."

Dad's advice in mind, I head back to the King's Highway.

8

SO, HERE'S WHAT I'M THINKING AS SOON AS I PULL ONTO Cherry Tree Road. Maybe it's not such a good idea to park right outside the house. For two reasons. First, if there's a killer out there and he has his eye on the house, I'd rather not advertise the fact that I'm inside the place all alone.

Second, I don't want the Cherry Tree residents to get suspicious. Last thing I need is nosy neighbors lobbing all sorts of questions about why I'm looking around the Girvin's old house all by my lonesome, even if it is the sight of some wrongdoing.

So, instead of parking outside the house itself, I hang a right onto Cherry Tree, pull over to the side of the road by a stand of old pines, and cut the ignition.

I hoof it on foot from there.

Standing outside on the street, the yellow crime scene ribbon pressed up against my knees, I get my first panoramic glance of the two-story structure from outside the confines of a motor vehicle. I take a long look at it's gabled roof, big French windows, second floor balcony off the garage (a new edition since the Civil War era), black shutters, and the old maple and pine trees that surround it. Digging my hand into my jacket pocket, I pull out the ring of keys Miller gave me, step over the ribbon, and swiftly make my way along the gravel driveway to the house.

I head around the back of the garage, find a wooded backyard, the landscaping unkempt and thick. It's as if during the time it took me to cover the thirty or so feet from the driveway to the backyard, I went from a quiet suburban neighborhood of 2015 to an era back in time where it took an army of keepers to hold back the growth of the upstate New York forest.

Bushwhacking my way through the tall grass, I come to the back door off the kitchen. It's an old, wood plank door that's been painted black, the wood so thick and old I would not doubt that it dates back to the time of Clara Harris and Henry Rathbone.

I push the key into the twentieth-century era lock. It takes some monkey grease to release the latch. That's when I pull the key back out and push the door open, the hinges creaking and squeaking. Stepping into the kitchen, I don't find the usual stainless steel paneled refrigerator or GE stove with computer programmable burners and glass countertop. No state-of-the-art microwave, no wine cooler, and no sign of a wet sink, to which might be attached a water-filtering spigot that can provide several varieties and intensity of sprays. No remote control retractable blinds over the windows. No dimmer switch for any LED track lighting. No digital, remotely programmable, local APD-connected security system.

There's no overhead electric lighting at all.

There is, however, a chandelier that sports a dozen or more candles that have burnt down to almost nothing. In place of a wet sink is a wooden water bucket that hangs by a pole mounted to the floor by the iron stove. There's also a working fireplace, the hearth of which is big enough for me to stand inside of. The floor is wood plank and warped in places. I breathe in the air. It smells of burnt candle wax, fire embers, and dust. It's summer, but there's a chill in the air as if the temperature inside the old house defies the seasons, surviving on its own timeline.

The chill gives me the willies to be perfectly honest. Spend enough time in creepy places like underground tombs and jungles that still contain the remnants of head-hunter tribesmen, and you learn to listen to your gut. And right now, my gut is telling me that this house which seems so cute and quaint from the outside is not a safe and happy place at all. A place where blood has not only been spilled but people have died. Violently.

I step through the door opening on the opposite side of the kitchen and enter into a small alcove. It's dark, so I pull a small LED flashlight from my bush jacket pocket, thumb the latex-covered trigger, and splash the brilliant light onto the walls.

The wood paneling is covered in photos. Old, metal-framed photos of what I guess to be the Girvin family...the man and wife who purchased the old home from Henry Rathbone and Clara Harris's son, Henry Jr. Probably somewhere around the early 1940s if I have to guess. It's odd because the photos aren't the color glossy you might expect. Rather, they're old black and whites that were taken by an old fashioned tripod-mounted box camera that might have been used by Mathew Brady back in the day. But then, given the information Miller passed on about the couple dedicating themselves to living the life of a civil war era couple, I shouldn't be all that taken aback.

In the first photo I come to, I make out a young Girvin and his wife at their wedding—her seated in a chair, dressed in a white gown and extra-long veil. Him dressed in a black suit with a collar buttoned half way up his neck, an old-fashioned bowtie perfectly knotted. He's sporting a thick, handlebar mustache, pork chop sideburns, and neither one of them are smiling since it would take far too much effort.

Another photo shows the young couple seated out back, the yard far more groomed than it is now. Girvin is wearing a long-sleeved shirt, the sleeves rolled up. She's wearing a long hoop skirt, a frilly blouse, and a hat covered with garden flowers. She's also holding a parasol against the hot summer sun. There's a third man in the photo. He's old, hunch-backed, his scalp bald while a thick white beard covers his face. His eyes are wet, forlorn, and scream of a man not long for this life. My gut tells me he is Henry Riggs Rathbone, Jr.

Yet another photo shows the Girvins standing outside the front door of the house beside a horse-drawn carriage. He's wearing a dark suit and she's wearing a long dress and matching jacket. She's also wearing long gloves. My guess is they're taking a trip somewhere. Maybe downtown Albany, which, in that horse-powered contraption, should have taken most of the day to make the round trip.

I pull the flashlight away, point it at the living room. A long couch occupies the center of the extended space, a wood harvest table pressed up against its back while an old dark wood coffee table is set in front of it. Beyond the coffee table is a fireplace which, from where I'm standing, looks like it sports some fresh embers. I'm wondering who would have made a fire as recently as a few hours ago if the Girvins have been missing for more than a week.

Aiming the flashlight above the fireplace's thick railroad tie mantle, I find a large painting hanging on the wall. It's a portrait of a young woman. She's attractive but sad, her lips frowning, her eyelids at half-mast. She's looking forlornly off to the right, not like she's eyeing anything in particular, but instead pondering the present condition of her life. Her hair is pinned up in the back, and she's wearing a dress with a flowery collar.

Stepping around the couch, past the coffee table, I shine the white light onto the small placard located at the bottom of the painting on the lower slat of the wooden frame. Embossed into the metal panel is the name, Clara Harris.

Just then I make out a knock...Or a snap.

Something colliding with wood. A foot maybe. A booted foot.

I turn quickly, shine the light out towards the alcove and the kitchen.

"Who's there?" I say aloud, my voice sounding strange and thin inside the seemingly empty space.

I wait, heart beating in my mouth. But I get nothing in response. Wait some more. But no more knocking sound.

"It's an old as all hell house," I whisper to myself. "Just a mouse."

It's as good an excuse as any, I guess. But I wish I had my .45 with me.

Exiting the living room, I enter into the vestibule which is covered in a throw rug that bears an American flag embroidered in its center. The states in the flag are represented by a circle of stars. Maybe twenty of them. As many states as might have existed during the Civil War. I guess I should know how many existed back then. But then, remember that C?

Directly above me hangs a chandelier powered by more candles, years and years of wax having melted and solidified on the wrought iron arms. Beyond that is a staircase that takes up the entirety of the far wall. I stand at the base of the stairs, looking up.

The hall at the top of the staircase is dark and foreboding. To my right is the dining room, a big empty table occupying its center, as are the ladder-backed chairs that surround it. Shining the LED light into the room, I make out yet another chandelier and more paintings hanging on the walls, including one that clearly depicts the Lincoln assassination at Ford's Theater.

The large rectangular painting draws me into the room until I stop myself maybe three feet away from its surface. The image is one I've seen probably two or three thousand times since childhood. The kind of illustration you might find in a grade school textbook. Only now, for the first time, the picture takes on new significance.

In the frame, we see Lincoln unknowingly seated in the Presidential box directly beside his wife, Mary. Behind him, John Wilkes Booth is firing his Derringer. The painting has captured the exact moment in time that the bullet is escaping the hand cannon and entering into the back of the President's cranial vault, the smoke from the exploded gunpowder billowing up from it. An American flag is draped over the right side of the box, its blue box of stars representing the "perfect union" providing a bitter backdrop for Booth while its opposite, striped end representing the thirteen original colonies, touches Lincoln's outstretched hand. The flag looks weary, sad, and defeated as if weeping for the death of her greatest President.

Meanwhile, positioned at the opposite side of the box are two individuals who, up until now, never gave me a second thought. They are Major Henry Rathbone and Clara Harris, the original owners of the house I now occupy. Clara sits beside Mary on her red velvet covered chair. Mary has yet to register the shot, her right hand holding a fan which is pressed against her heart. The expression on Clara's face clearly indicates some kind of confusion. That the shot has indeed registered with her, but only just slightly.

However, raising himself out of his chair directly beside her is her fiancé, Henry. Dressed in his uniform blues, he knows precisely what's happening. True to form for a man of action, he has bounded up, his left arm fully extended, his hand trying desperately to reach out for the assassin as he murder's the President.

For the first time ever, I feel myself more drawn into the drama of Clara and Henry than Abraham and Mary if only because of the drama and sadness they inherited just by becoming victims of tragic circumstances. While Clara is shocked and even disbelieving of the events happening before her eyes, Henry, a combat veteran, believes entirely in what he is witnessing and is doing his best to stop it.

As if to prove it, only a second or two after this moment captured in time, Henry will lunge after Booth and pay dearly for his selfless actions with a deep laceration on his arm from elbow to shoulder. But, as I peer at the illustration and the drama being played out before my eyes, I finally recognize the significance of the moment captured in time. It's this severe wounding of Rathbone that will allow Booth to get away with murder. A situation that will cause far more scarring to Rathbone than a knife cut ever could. A situation that will haunt him for the rest of his days to the point of madness, murder, and suicide.

A curse? Nah, just bad luck...

"Poor, poor, bastard," I whisper to myself inside the old, musty home.

Pulling my eyes from the painting, I head back into the vestibule and face the staircase. Heart pumping in my throat, I start to climb.

9

THE STAIRS CREAK WITH MY EVERY FOOTSTEP AS IF CRYING out in pain. The wood treads are so dry and old it wouldn't take more than a fleeting spark to light them up. I glance over my shoulder at the chandelier and candles that are burned down to almost nothing and I can't believe this place isn't already a pile of charred embers.

Coming to the top of the stairs, I step out onto the landing and shine the flashlight down the short corridor. With the place having been shuttered, and minimal air circulating through the upper level, the dust that's settled is upset with my every slow step along the narrow, wood plank floor. In the LED light, the dust looks like a miniature Milky Way of stars revolving around the sun.

There are only two doors. One to my right and one to my left.

I open the one to my right and step inside. I spot a metal-framed bed with metal end tables positioned on both sides, each of which support a kerosene lamp. A tall dresser of drawers is pushed up against the wall, and a night table with attached mirror, the glass old and warped, is set beside it. Placed before the mirror is a wash basin, a washcloth, an old fashioned toothbrush—possibly carved from ivory, tooth powder, and a comb. I also make out a straight razor, some cologne, and hair putty. Bill Girvin's room, no doubt.

Stepping back out of the room, I cross the hall and enter into what I take to be Mrs. Girvin's room...the bedroom that, in my mind anyway, formerly belonged to Clara Harris. It's no secret that married couples of the nineteenth century practiced birth control by sleeping in separate bedrooms. In the twenty-first century, we have electronically adjustable king-sized beds and the morning after pill.

Slowly, almost tentatively, I push the door open, careful not to step inside right away, as if there's somebody inside waiting for me. Waiting to pounce on me.

Paranoia?

Maybe.

Or maybe I'm just spooked. Truth is, the more time I spend in this place, the more spooked I feel. It's not because of the noise I heard downstairs...a noise which could be explained by a thousand different things—mice being the least of them. It's because the crap detector in my gut is nudging me, telling me to watch my back, that the sensation of being watched by either ghost or the real flesh and blood thing (or both) is not just paranoia, but an all too real possibility.

I step inside, spot Mrs. Girvin's bed. It's a sleigh bed, the frame a dark walnut. The mattress looks almost as old as the frame, the feather-stuffed mattress sunken down in the center from years of overuse. Maybe I'm not looking at Mrs. Girvin's bed at all, but Clara's. Whatever the case, I can only imagine the generations of bugs that have assumed squatters rights inside the thing.

There's something else occupying the bed.

A blood stain.

In the light from the LED lantern, I can see that the circular stain is fresh and crimson colored. One, or both, Girvins lost blood here before disappearing. According to Miller, that is. It dawns on me then that if one or both Girvins were bleeding that badly, their blood would have stained the entire house. Drops and smears would be on the floorboards, the walls, the banister, on the staircase...everywhere. But it's only on the bed.

I scan the bedroom with the flashlight.

Like her husband's bedroom, the bed is bookended by kerosene lamps, the glass shells partially blackened from years of use. To my left is a dresser of drawers and set beside it, diagonally in the corner is a dressing table and mirror. There's a porcelain wash basin and a towel, as well as a comb made of bone, and a brush.

To the right is the double-hung window, the heavy fabric drapes closed, the sun's brilliant mid-day radiance entirely blocked. I find myself shaking my head. Who in their right mind willingly decides to give up all modern conveniences for a life of solitude and inconvenience? But then, who am I to judge? I've slept in some strange places myself. A two floor, concrete block hostel located in the middle of the Amazon Basin comes to mind. My second floor room contained a ceiling fan and mattress with a sweat stain on it that mimicked the shape of a human body. The wall behind the bed was covered in blood spatter as if someone had kicked the door in on some unsuspecting son of a bitch and sprayed him with lead where he lay.

I shift myself to the right and find the closet door.

My stomach jumps. Heart beats. The built-in crap detector is smelling something. Something hidden.

The curse...

"This must be the one," I whisper.

I open the closet door, push aside the clothing that hangs on the metal bar. Shining the LED lantern onto the back wall, my heart sinks down to my feet. All that's visible is an old plaster and lath wall. The brick wall isn't here.

"What if it's in old man Girvin's room?" I whisper to myself, crossing the hall back into his bedroom.

I head to the closet, open the wood door. No brick wall there either.

There are two other bedrooms further down the hall. I head into each of them, examining the closets. No brick walls.

Out in the hallway, I have a one man huddle with myself.

"Okay," I say aloud, my voice sounding hollow and odd inside the empty hall. "According to Balkis and Miller, legend has it that the dress was hidden behind a brick wall in Clara's bedroom closet. That closet is now Mrs. Girvin's closet and has been for decades and decades. So why then, no bricks?"

Then it comes to me that I'm simply looking in the wrong place. That maybe the legend isn't quite right, as legends have a nasty habit of being. What if the wall exists, but it's just not where it's supposed to be?

That question clearly in mind, I head back into Clara's bedroom.

10

I TAKE ANOTHER LOOK AROUND THE ROOM, SHINING THE flashlight on the walls, the ceiling, the floor. I go to the opposite end of the room, begin rapping the wall with my knuckles, knowing that should a brick wall exist behind the plaster, my skin and bone will detect the more rigid material. I make my way around the room, and manage only to come up with hollow knocks.

Once more, I shine the light onto the ceiling.

"That's way too impractical," I whisper to myself.

That's when, once more, I shine the light on the floor. My gut speaks to me then. Screams is more like it.

"Jesus," I say. "I should have thought of this ages ago."

Crouching, I press both hands against the big sleigh bed like it's a blocking sled from my high school football days, and begin to push. It's so heavy and cumbersome, the bed seems bolted to the floor. After three hard shoves, I manage to move it all the way to the opposite wall. Looking down at the floor, I see something that confirms my suspicions.

A piece of perfectly square flooring that's looks to have been cut out and reinstalled at a later date. Taking a knee, I feel around the four by four foot square portion with my bare hands. The thin joint is filled with dirt and dust. I can hardly even jam my fingernails into the thin separation, much less shove my fingers inside.

A crowbar would be nice right about now. But I don't have one.

"There's always the kitchen," I whisper.

Back up on my feet, I head back down to the kitchen in the hope of finding a knife that's big enough to cut through Clara's floor.

Moments later, I'm back upstairs in the bedroom a heavy meat cleaver in hand. The sucker must weigh five pounds it's so big. By the looks of the steel blade, it couldn't bring down a tree much less butcher a pig into a few dozen pork chops.

Taking a knee, I raise up the cutting edge and, aiming for the joint, swing it rapidly downwards and connect with the wood. I don't hit the joint exactly, but the blade lands close enough to cause a chunk of the old dried wood to shatter. Pulling the knife out, I raise it and swing again, more of the wood disintegrating as I chop. After a few minutes of this, I've created an opening big enough for me to reach in with my hands. That's when I begin to pull the pieces of floorboard up. In no time at all, I've removed almost the entirety of the square area.

Pulse pounding, I pull the flashlight from my pocket, shine it down into the opening. That's when I see it—a wooden staircase covered in cobwebs and dust that contains maybe a half dozen risers. What's located at the bottom of this staircase steals my breath away.

I don't see plaster-covered lath. Instead, I see something else.

A brick wall.

My crap detector whispers something to me. My heart begins to beat in my temples. The hairs on the back of my neck stand at attention as I feel the eyes upon me. The eyes of a ghost. Lincoln's spirit? His eyes? Clara and Henry's eyes? The butcher knife in hand, I stand and scan the sleigh bed once more with the flashlight, eye the blood stain.

Nothing there.

Quickly, I make my way over to the sleigh bed, push myself between the frame and the exterior wall. Using all my strength, I shove the bed back over the opening in the floor. Then, coming around to the opposite side of the mattress, I shine the light directly into the mirror on the table in the corner. That's when I see myself...

...and something else.

The bedroom door opening and a mustached man dressed in a white shirt stepping inside.

I turn quick...

11

THE PRESIDENTIAL BOX IS SMALL, NARROW, AND BARELY *fits four chairs and the adults who occupy them.*

I'm seated in the chair furthest away from the man I most revere in the world. The man I would have taken a bullet for on the field of battle be it Manassas, Shiloh, Gettysburg...

...Gettysburg.

I was there that day when he spoke. I stood close to a cobbed wood podium that gave his already extraordinary height even more verticality. Add to that his tall top hat, and he appeared not like a mortal man at all but a giant born not of this earth. But then, the man is a giant among men. A sad giant at that. A man who doesn't fit into this world in this day and age. A man who seems too big for his own pale skin and bones.

I try not to stare at him as he sits in his chair at the

far end of the box by the wood door, his hands laid flat on his knees, the sleeves on his charcoal jacket too short so that his bony wrists are exposed, the backs of his hands crisscrossed with thick purple veins, fingers long, crooked, and painful looking. Like old dry twigs in the dead of winter.

It doesn't take a genius to recognize the exhaustion in him. It's never more apparent than on his face—long, cracked, and sunken like a piece of old fractured window glass that has drooped with time. His black beard is speckled with gray and it sings not of age, but instead of impending doom.

Once, when I seem to have forgotten my manners, I lock eyes on him as the skin-tagged eyelids slowly descend and sleep begins to overwhelm him, his chin coming within a hair's length of his sternum. But just before chin connects with chest, his internal alarm awakens him like the loudest of roosters.

His eyes pop open wide.

I almost want to laugh aloud, but dare not. But then something happens that sends a start into my heart. He connects with my gaze as if he knew I was eyeing him the whole time. Almost as if he was putting on a show for me far more interesting than the one currently playing on the stage below.

The truth: I feel the embarrassment well up on my face in the form of blood. The President is a strong man but a kind man, too. And he issues me the gentlest of the smiles as if to say, "It's okay, young man. I don't blame you for eavesdropping."

Quickly turning my head then, I try to concentrate on the play. But such affairs fill me with the utmost disinterest if not dread. Like a household chore that must be accomplished whether I like it or not. Oh, the things we must do for those we love the most.

The one I love most...I shift my eyes towards her. My Clara. I'm seated in my chair like a proper gentleman, but if only we were all alone in this box. It might be possible for me to wrap my arms around her, caress the soft skin on her face, run my hands through her thick hair, kiss her tender lips. Oh, how I am counting the days until we wed, when it will be possible to lie ourselves down together in our marriage bed, without the burden of our clothing, our naked bodies pressed together, tightly, sweetly, lovingly.

The box door opens slowly.

So slowly, the movement of wood slab on well-oiled hinges barely registers. Which means I hardly take notice. Initially, I'm of the opinion that one of Lincoln's sleepy guards is delivering a message to him as can happen from time to time, even during performances such as this one that are dear to Mrs. Lincoln.

Yet, the man entering quietly, but somehow deliberately, into the box is no blue-uniformed guard. He is, instead, a tall, mustached, dark-haired man who bears the handsome face of an actor. I have seen this face before. Both on poster advertisements and in the newspapers. His name, however, escapes me as he raises up his right hand to reveal something inside it.

It's a pistol.

A small pistol that I recognize right away. A Derringer or what's known as a pocket cannon. When he aims the barrel of the weapon at the back of the President's skull, I know precisely what is about to follow. Yet, for some reason, the reality of the situation begins to escape me. It's as if this man's actions...this actor...were playing a part in a separate play altogether or perhaps acting out a scene which is meant to distract from the main scene being revealed on the stage. How inventive and yet odd that the President has chosen to portray himself in a stage play so soon after the war against Southern aggression has ceased.

A comedic line is delivered on stage. It causes the audience to erupt in laughter. Even Mr. Lincoln goes wide-eyed while issuing a heartfelt series of giggles.

Then the shot.

The explosive concussion reverberates throughout the playhouse and all manner of make-believe is wiped away in the instant it takes for Lincoln's cerebral blood to spatter over both Mary's and Clara's dresses, the latter of which is pearl white. Lincoln's head thrusts forward, chin against sternum, not unlike his bouts of fatigue. But this time, the bobbing is violent and severe. I raise my left arm, reaching out for the killer with open hands, as the President slumps into his own lap. But I can't possibly reach him, separated as I am from him by two grown women.

Clara turns, looks on in horror, while Mary continues to gaze upon the play like the surreal moment is having trouble registering in her brain. The collective gasp of the crowd fills the deadly silence when I make a desperate lunge for the man as if attacking an entrenched enemy Rebel.

Clara screams. Mary wails and takes hold of her husband, setting her left hand on the back of his head as if trying to put the shattered egg of a skull back together again.

I manage to grab the killer's sleeve on his shooting arm. From there, I regain my balance and shift my grip to his forearm. I am just about to physically subdue him with the utmost strength in my body, when his left hand comes up revealing a dagger. He is quick with the weapon, slicing my left arm from elbow to shoulder. The cut is so swiftly and expertly applied that the pain is minimal if non-existent. All that registers is the immediate loss of blood, a dizziness in my brain, and a sickness in my stomach. I go down on my knees and wretch an ugly mixture of sputum and bile while Clara comes to my aid, grabbing my collar.

"I have done it! I have avenged the Confederacy!" shouts the booming, stage-trained voice of the killer after pulling himself away from me and leaping out of the box onto the stage. "Sic Semper Tyrannus!"

"My husband!" Mary Lincoln shrieks. "Someone help my husband!"

But all I can think about as the world around me fades to darkness, is Clara's dress.

"You're ruining your dress, my love," I whisper. "It's covered in blood and it's all my fault."

12

WHEN I COME TO, I'M CHAINED AND SHACKLED INSIDE A dark, dank, colorless hell hole that smells like mold, must, and cat piss. Shaking the webs out of my pounding head, I realize I'm sitting inside the stone-walled basement of this old home. A basement that resembles—in my battered brain anyway—a dungeon or, more accurately, a Civil War-era prison.

Between the bizarre dream where I assumed the role of Major Henry Rathbone and this dark, dank place, I feel as if I've been transported back in time.

The place0is half-lit with kerosene lamps positioned on wood tables. A couple of wall-mounted wood torches are also burning, giving off a red-orange glow. I'm still fully clothed, my bush jacket still draping my torso. That's a good sign. If my wrists weren't shackled, I'd dig into my pocket for my Swiss Army Knife. My mind begins to run through ways to free myself. I scan the area around me for anything that might help. That's when I realize something...

I'm not alone.

As my eyes regain their focus, I can make out the figure of a man standing on the opposite side of the square space. His face is shadowed, but he's wearing a suit with a long coat over a white shirt, an ascot, straight trousers, and riding boots. He sees I'm awake and approaches me. As he comes closer, I can tell that the man is Balkis but he's pretending to be somebody else. If I had to guess, he's playing the role of John Wilkes Booth. His manner of dress taken together with his long black wavy hair and overly thick handlebar mustache are dead giveaways.

"I knew you were an asshole from the moment I met you, Balkis," I say, the words feeling as if they're peeling themselves away from the back of my throat. "But I didn't know you were this much of a pathological asshole."

He slowly bends at the knees, backhands me across the mouth. My head spins and I taste the iron of my blood on my now split upper lip. When I get a hold of this lunatic—and I *will* get ahold of him if it's the last thing I do—I'm gonna break his nose.

"Silence, Yankee scum," he barks. "I will do the talking."

"Maybe you should put some duct tape over my mouth."

"What, pray tell, is this duct tape you speak of?"

Who exactly is this lunatic and how did I end up inside this place?

"Cut the shit, Balkis--"

"Stop!" He raises his right hand in a dramatic, actor-like fashion. "Who is this Balkis?"

"It's you, dummy. The madman who cold-cocked me upstairs."

"I am not that man. You know me as John Wilkes Booth."

I'm sure I'm smiling. Because I can feel the muscles in my face tightening, contracting.

Me laughing aloud.

He bitch slaps me again.

I yank on the shackles, the sound of metal slapping against the stone wall filling the square space. To no avail.

"Okay, Balkis...ummm, excuse me...Mr. Booth. What's this all about? You kill the Girvins and bury them somewhere? Did you do it so you could somehow lay claim to their house and the dress that might be hidden inside it? There a deed somewhere with your name newly printed on it? What did you promise the Girvins to convince them to sign the joint over to you? Did you tell them that you and you alone represented the university? Fool them into believing it? And once that was done and they realized they'd been duped, you killed them in your rather, ummm, dramatic fashion using the same weapons the real Booth used to kill Lincoln?"

His eyes go wide. "I know nothing of which you speak, Yankee."

Another slap. This one hard enough to make my eyes water. "What fucking planet are you from?"

The hand raised again.

"Wait...wait...wait, Mr. Booth. I apologize. I'm really, really sorry about how things turned out in the war and I think you had every right to shoot Lincoln in the head."

He slowly lowers his hand, relaxes his grip. "That meddling man did not only destroy the Southern union, he destroyed a way of life, and an entire people."

"This isn't about slavery, is it?"

"Of course not. Man has a right to own slaves if he wishes. This is more about one man believing he is above the law and the Constitution of the United States of America. That was your Mr. Lincoln."

"So, what exactly do you want of me?"

"You, Mr. Baker, are going to dig up Clara's dress for me."

"Why do you want it, Mr. Booth? It contains the spilled blood of Lincoln and Henry Rathbone. Won't it repulse you to be in the possession of something so closely linked with the men you must abhor the most on this flat earth?"

"On the contrary, Mr. Baker, that dress is no longer of this earth. It is a direct link to Lincoln and his spirit. If I possess the dress, I possess the ability to reverse the curse and haunt the man's spirit for all eternity. But first, you must find it for me."

Reverse the curse...

Okay, stop the damn train because I wanna get off. What I mean is, I've run into a few lunatics over the course of my career, but this guy takes the cake and the platter it was served on, too. Call in the white coats!

"The dress doesn't exist. Clara's son burned it, remember?"

"A wives' tale to be sure. The dress was too important. Too haunted. Too powerful to be burned. Had her boy attempted to put a lit match to it, he would have been exposed to the curse and suffered a great injury. Something fatal and ugly. As it is, he lived a long, healthy life which means he went nowhere near the cursed dress."

Upstairs in Clara's bedroom closet...The brick wall...It's still there...But Balkis/Booth doesn't know about the hole in the bedroom floor.

I think it over for a minute. Clearly this man is out of his gourd. Nuts. Beyond nuts. On the way to the looney bin crazy. But I'm shackled to a stone wall. And if I ever expect to be unshackled, I should probably play along with his ridiculous game of partnering up with John Wilkes Booth to find Clara's ancient dress.

"Okay," I say.

"Okay what, Mr. Baker?"

"Okay, I'll help you, Mr. Booth."

He pauses a moment, grows a crafty grin.

"I see now," he says, his voice hardly more than a whisper.

"See what, whack job?"

The backhand that wallops the left side of my face doesn't hurt anymore. It just pisses me off further.

"How long shall we keep this up, Mr. Baker? Until I break your jaw? Or perhaps knock out a tooth?"

"Sorry," I say. "As you were saying...Mr. Booth?"

"I said, I see. As in, I see what you are up to. You wish to work with me in order that I unshackle you, and once that's done, you will do your best to bring physical harm to my person. And that, I'm afraid, I cannot allow."

Okay, so he's on to me. He might be a total looney, but he's not as dumb as I thought. Still, he needs to unshackle me if I'm to help him out.

"So what are your suggestions?" I say. "I help you out by using mental telepathy?"

"Not at all." He smiles. Then, "On your knees."

Staring into his big brown eyes. "Why?"

"Because I said so."

"Sic Semper Tyrannus," I whisper.

"Excuse me, sir?"

"Oh," I say. "I, uhh, can't wait to see what your sick plan is, Mr. Booth."

Shifting onto my knees carefully without breaking

my wrists against the shackles, he backsteps into the darker recesses of the basement-slash-dungeon, messes with something laid out on a table, carries it back over to me. What I see takes me by complete surprise, considering this man is supposed to be caught up in some sort of bizarre *Twilight Zone* time warp. It's a belt loaded with plastic explosive.

"Allow me, please," he says, wrapping the belt around my waist, buckling it tightly against my lower spine.

Well, I'll be a dumb son of a bitch. Balkis might not be dealing with reality, but he certainly knows how to raise the stakes. He pulls a good old-fashioned skeleton key from the pocket of his trousers and unlocks each of my wrists.

As I stand, he holds out something that looks like a smartphone. That's because it is a smartphone. How odd it appears in the hand of some reenactment aficionado flashback from 1865. And to think he pretended to never hear of duct tape.

"One false move," he explains. "One single attempt at running away, or to do me physical harm, and I will punch the single digit that will blow you straight to the kingdom of hell along with Mr. Lincoln. Do I make myself clear?"

He could be bluffing, of course. The stuff wrapped around my waist might be Play Dough for all I know. But I feel the weight of the belt against my torso, and I have no reason *not* to believe it's the real deal. C-4, which, if detonated, would not simply cut me in two. It would pretty much evaporate me.

"Very clear, Mr. Booth," I say.

"We shall commence our work together," he says. "Now tell me, Mr. Baker, what exactly were you doing in Clara Harris's bedroom prior to my walking in on you?"

13

I PONDER THE QUESTION FOR A MOMENT.

Why not just be honest with him, Baker, and admit you found the brick wall?

Taking a careful, non-threatening step forward, I say, "I found it, Booth. I found the wall."

His face lights up like a lamp.

"But let me ask you something first," I go on. "In all the years the Girvin's lived here, before their unfortunate...ummm...disappearance, didn't they search the joint for the dress?"

What I really want to ask Balkis is if he chained them up down in the basement, put a gun to their heads and tried to make them talk. But I'm in no position to start lobbing accusations with enough explosive wrapped around my mid-section to force doctors to ID me by my teeth should I piss him off sufficiently.

"Alas," he says, raising his eyes up to the dark, rough wood ceiling, as if looking through the timbers to heaven, "it's possible the Girvins searched their entire lives and in the end, decided to believe in the legend. That Henry Riggs Rathbone Jr. did indeed break down the brick wall you speak of, take possession of the dress, and burn it." His lit face burns even brighter. Then, "Clearly my instincts have served me right in selecting you to find Clara's relic. It would be a shame to have to blow you up."

"I'll do my best to serve the cause," I say. "Besides, who needs all that mess?"

14

WE TRUDGE OUR WAY BACK UP TWO FLIGHTS OF STAIRS.
Me and all the death wrapped around my waist, and
Balkis aka John Wilkes Booth with his smartphone
stuffed in his trouser pocket and a five pound mash
hammer gripped in his right hand. Heart beating in my
throat, I take the lead while Balkis remains a good five
or six steps behind me. Makes me think that if the time
comes to blow me to smithereens, he'll be able to place
as much distance between "me and thee" as possible in
as brief amount of time as possible.

At the top of the stairs I head into a short corridor
and hook a left into Clara's bedroom where, not too long
ago, Balkis knocked me cold. Why Balkis felt compelled
to drag me down into that dungeon in the first place is
anybody's guess. But I'm sure dramatics had something
to do with it. He is the civil war reenactor after all.

Together, we push the bed out of the way, stand before the hole in the floor.

Meantime, I await his direction.

He hands me the mash hammer. At the same time, he pulls out his smartphone, positions his thumb on the particular nasty digit.

"I'm going to assume you're smarter than that," he says, shooting a glance at the weighty mash hammer.

Out the corner of my eye, I see the butcher knife on the floor. Again, he's nuts, but he's sharper than I thought because he sees me eyeing the knife.

He bursts out laughing.

"Don't even think about it, Baker," he says, shifting himself over to the spot where the knife sits on the floor. He bends at the knees, picks the blade up, walks it over to the window where he pulls back the curtain. Breaking one of the panes with the blade, he then tosses it out the opening.

Crap. No more knife...

The heart pulsing in my throat is now accompanied by a dry mouth and beads of sweat on my brow.

"Down the stairs please," he says.

Turning back to Booth/Balkis.

"I need a light," I say, remembering my small LED light that's now AWOL. "A flashlight."

At first, he shoots a look over his shoulder at the kerosene lamp. Then he issues an aggravated exhale while punching a couple of commands into the smartphone which initiates an LED flashlight app.

I hold my breath while a shot of ice cold chill shoots up and down my spine.

Christ almighty, what if he mistakenly hits the wrong digit?

Of course, I wouldn't know what hit me should that happen. Or so I can only hope.

"Down the stairs," he repeats. "I'll be right behind you."

He shines the light onto the opening. It illuminates both the staircase and the brick wall. Inhaling a breath, I step down onto the first tread. The board squeaks and strains, but seems strong enough. Taking it slowly, I descend all six stairs, the thick spider webs breaking against my face, until I face the brick wall.

Balkis follows, that LED smartphone light shining on the wall the entire time.

Pulse picks up speed.

Maybe the dress is inside the closet after all. But then, I can't rid myself of the persistent twenty thousand dollar question: Why hadn't the Girvin's thought to break through the floor and the wall in the search of the dress?

It's a question I once again pose to Balkis.

He douses the LED light. "The Girvins were spooked by this brick wall and what it might hide."

"In all the decades they lived here, they're curiosity didn't override the spookiness? Not even once?" I ask.

"It was a question of being careful of what you wish for."

"Excuse me?"

"The Girvins never really *wanted* to find Clara's dress, Mr. Baker. They spoke a good game about finding what, in essence, might be one of the most prized Lincoln relics ever to be discovered. But to them, finding the dress would be like opening a Pandora's Box."

The curse...

"Why didn't you just sneak into the house, make an effort to find the wall, and break it down yourself? You didn't need me to find it."

He shakes his head.

"I thought of that a hundred times. But searching

the house for the wall wouldn't be easy. The Girvins were permanent fixtures of the place and Mrs. Girvin always locked both the closet and her room whenever she wasn't inside them. It would be impossible to break in without their knowing. And now that I know the brick wall wasn't located in the closet at all, but under the floor, surely they would have tried to stop me."

"They're old and infirmed...Or, were old and infirmed anyway. You could have walked right past them and headed upstairs and they might not have known."

He shakes his head.

"The old man, Mr. Girvin, he's more with it than you think. He would have shot me on the spot if I went anywhere near Clara's bedroom. He's not only a gun owner, but he often carried a pistol on his person even while in the house. Sometimes he carried a rifle too. They were that fearful of the modern world outside their home. A world they viewed with paranoia. And as the years passed, they came to be even more terrified of the dress. If I were to expose it to them, they would be haunted for all their days, just like Clara and Henry before them."

That's when it dawns on me. Balkis is also afraid of the curse. Which is precisely why he's making me do the dirty work by digging it up...so to speak.

"Turns out the Girvin's days were numbered anyway," I say, knowing I probably shouldn't have.

Balkis/Booth once more shifts his thumb so that it rests on the nasty digit.

"As much as you'd like to believe Dr. Balkis killed the Girvins, you couldn't be more wrong, Mr. Baker."

"I get the message, Mr. Booth," I add.

"Mr. Baker, tear down that wall."

Screw the Lincoln Curse and the horse it rode in on...

Raising the mash hammer, I strike at the brick.

15

THE BRICK CRUMBLES.

A small hole appears.

"More, Baker," Balkis/Booth says, his voice trembling with excitement. "Break more of it down."

He doesn't have to tell me twice. I'm an explorer after all. A sandhog. Even with a bomb wrapped around my belly, I need to see what's behind the wall as much as he does.

I pound more of it out. Almost immediately a cool, stale, moldy odor slaps our faces.

"The light," I say. "I think I see it. I think I see the dress, Booth."

"It's true," he says. "It was here all the time. I just needed the Girvins out of the way."

With a trembling hand, he turns his LED light back on, shines it inside.

"God almighty it's true," he repeats, now apparently unconcerned with the curse. "Where is it?"

"Closer," I insist. "Move in closer with the light. It's right there, glowing as if the ghost of Clara is still wearing it. It's the most beautiful apparition I've ever seen."

He holds the light inside the opening, his eyes peeled onto the empty space. That's when I crack the son of a bitch over the head with the mash hammer.

16

HE GOES DOWN HARD, THE SMARTPHONE LANDING INSIDE the broken wall. Rather, not landing on a floor, but falling down what sounds to me like a series of iron steps.

I pat him down, find he's unarmed. Reaching around back, I unbuckle the bomb belt, set it to the side. I dig into my pocket, find my Swiss Army knife, open the blade. Gently, I slit the translucent plastic on the first piece of C-4. Taking a sniff of the material, I recognize the smell easily enough. Part sweet, part sour. You're everyday construction putty.

The C-4 belt was a fake.

Go figure...

Balkis is not only nutty, he's psychopathic phony. I head up the steps to Clara's water basin and discover there's still water inside it.

I carry it back to Balkis, stand at the edge of the square opening and pour it over his mustached face.

He comes to in a fit of spitting and coughing.

"What has thou done to me?" he says.

"Cut the shit, you crazy bastard," I say. "The show's over which means you can stop talking like somebody you're not. This ain't no reenactment."

"What happened?"

"I'm smarter than you is what happened. You're lucky the police aren't dragging your psychotic ass to prison right this second...*Ball-Kiss.*"

"You don't have to mock, Baker," he says, his voice returning to its normal contemporary whine, his face deflated if not defeated.

He sits up, shakes his head. "Where's my damned phone? I've already lost two this year alone."

"You'll see what happened to your phone in just a second."

Stepping over to Clara's bed lamp, I grab a box of wood matches from beside the old kerosene fixture and light it up. I carry it over to the hole in the floor, careful to step over Balkis' crumpled, chubby body. Making the steps back down to the brick wall, I hold the lamp inside the opening. I become witness to the reason the professor's smartphone seemed to bounce down a series of steps. Hidden behind the wall is not Clara's dress, but a spiral staircase.

17

BALKIS MANAGES TO PICK HIMSELF UP.

"My Lord, a staircase," he says, stating the obvious. "But where does it lead?"

"That's the question isn't it, asshole?"

"Please don't call me that, Baker," he says. "Besides..." His thought trails off.

"Besides what?"

"You're not about to call the police or beat me up or anything else."

"And why's that?"

"Because you want to see where that staircase leads as much as I do."

Crazy's got a point...

"Okay, Professor," I say, the lit kerosene lamp in hand. "But tell you what. You try anymore stunts, I will knock your teeth down your throat and feed your eyeballs to the neighborhood dogs. Do I make myself clear?"

Bending at the knees, I pick up the mash hammer. Then, I hand Balkis the lamp.

"You take the lead."

"Do I have a choice?"

"Funny," I say. "Now walk."

He just stands there.

I hold up the mash hammer like I'm going to hit him over the head with it again.

"Okay, okay," he says, raising the kerosene lamp so that it's at chest height, its dim light reflecting off of the old lath and plaster walls.

He begins descending the circular staircase one step at a time. I follow, taking each step carefully as though at any moment the old rusted iron treads might snap in two. Judging by the way the old staircase creaks, trembles, and cries out from the strain, that's not a far-out assumption.

The fetid odor grows more intense with each step downward. Stale combined with a sweetness that's not entirely unfamiliar. The air is cooler, too, which makes me believe we're heading down into an area that is more subterranean than the basement where I was locked up earlier.

When Balkis reaches the bottom, his shadow stretches out across a hard dirt floor that leads into a narrow room.

"Sweet baby Jesus in heaven," he says, as I negotiate the last step and lock my eyes on the dim, kerosene lamp-lit interior of the room and the two bodies it contains.

"Yes," I say, the mash hammer dropping out of my hand, "if heaven only knew."

18

THEY ARE LYING ON THE FLOOR WHICH IS COVERED WITH a rug that, over the decades, has mostly decayed and rotted from ground moisture. The woman and man are lying on their side, facing one another as if they've just laid down in their queen-sized Serta for the night. Their bodies have been reduced to skeletons, but their clothing has somehow been spared the ravages of time, as if the underground tomb and the thick rug beneath them, has managed to protect them from the elements.

Set on the floor in between them is a pistol. What I recognize as a Model 1858 Remington Army issue six-shooter. Despite the layer of dust that shrouds it, the pistol looks in good enough shape to shoot.

Balkis bends at the knees, picks up his smartphone, pockets it. He then takes a couple of steps forward, illuminating their figures in lamplight.

"Clara and Henry," he whispers, as if speaking aloud will somehow wake them up.

I approach them, stopping only when I come to their feet. Her's covered in high-heeled, lace-up shoes. His covered in leather riding boots.

"So the murder/suicide theory is true after all," I say. "But he didn't shoot her with Booth's Derringer and he didn't stab himself in the gut. He shot her first, then shot himself, down here in this dungeon."

"How can you tell?" Balkis says.

"You see where the pistol rests on the floor, less than an inch from that nickel-sized hole in Henry's forehead, his finger still on the trigger. He shot her in the heart and then himself in the head, using his left hand. Looks like his hand fell along with the gun and has remained in place ever since."

We both gaze upon the bodies in the ghostly golden lamplight. Although dead and decayed, there still seems to be a love between them. A love and emotion that remains palpable after all these years. That sweetness I smelled at the top of the staircase wasn't just the familiar scent of death...it was also one of love. A love that still somehow exists between Clara and Henry. A love that was almost destroyed by the blood and the ghost of a man who was assassinated for something he believed in and who spilled his sad life all over Clara's white dress. A love that is completely missing in the legendary accounts that attest to Henry having killed Clara over suspicion, paranoia, and anger.

Clara's dress...

With Balkis holding up the lamp, I make a three-hundred-sixty-degree examination of the room on the balls of my feet.

"The dress isn't here," I say, almost under my breath.

Balkis sidesteps to the stone wall, begins patting it with his free hand.

"Perhaps it's hidden in some secret chamber or compartment."

I shake my head.

"My gut tells me it's not here. That it was once here. But it's not here anymore. Because it wouldn't be hidden from view. Henry and Clara would no longer have any reason to keep it hidden. If it was the prime source of their obsession, it would be set out as plainly as their bodies."

He turns to me, his face glowing in the yellow-gold kerosene light.

"Henry Riggs Rathbone, Jr.," Balkis says.

"He must have removed the dress after finding his parents dead. That must be when he bricked up the closet so that no one would ever find them, or the dress that drove them to their graves. When he buried his parents, their coffins were empty...and empty they remain."

Balkis' face goes south. "So he did burn the dress after all."

Me, stealing a moment not to think necessarily, but to listen to my intuition. My gut. In my head, I see a younger version of the old, almost crippled man standing with the young Girvins outside the house. A man of maybe nineteen or twenty on his hands and knees, bricking up the closet opening and nailing down the floorboards so that no one would ever know of the subterranean room and the cursed human remains it contained.

"I don't think so, Professor Balkis," I say, after a time. "In fact, I know so."

"How do you know?"

I punch my own stomach.

"I can feel it right here. Feel the dress's presence. You see, like the Girvins who lived here after the Rathbones, I think it's possible old Henry Junior was afraid of what might happen should he attempt to destroy the dress. Afraid that he, too, might be haunted by the curse for the rest of his days."

"Why do you think he bricked his parents up instead of giving them a proper burial?"

I shake my head. "It must have had something to do with the curse. Disturb the dead, and disturb the curse."

"But what happened to the damn dress? The source of the curse."

"It's possible Clara and Henry had the dress with them when they died. Maybe after discovering his parent's bodies, a very spooked Henry grabbed hold of the dress and decided to do something else with it. Like get it out of the house for a change."

"So, where can the dress be then? Is it possible the Girvin's finally located it inside some old box and took off with it?"

"You tell me?" I say.

He shakes his head, purses his lips.

"I think not," he says. "Even if they had stumbled upon it somehow, they were far too afraid of its powers to even go near it."

I turn back to the bodies. My eyes lock on their skull faces staring eternally into one another. At their fetal positions, at their love for one another even in the face of violent death.

"Some things you just can't fight while you're alive. Some things you need to take with you to the afterlife in order to protect it. And to protect others from it."

"What on God's earth are you talking about, Baker?"

Me, turning back to Balkis.

"I can bet you a full year's salary, Professor, that if

we manage to find the Rathbone cemetery plots, we also find the Lincoln dress. We'll start with Henry Junior's grave first."

19

WE HEAD BACK UP THE SPIRAL STAIRCASE AND EXIT THE secret subterranean space through the hole in the floor. Once back inside Clara's old bedroom, Balkis returns the lamp to the bed stand, blows it out.

"You're the historian, Balkis," I say. "Where's Junior buried?"

He smiles. "I've already told you. Less than a mile away in the Albany Rural Cemetery. Have you wheels, Mr. Baker?"

"My rental truck's parked down the road."

"What are we waiting for?"

I hold out my hand, press it flat against the professor's bulging sternum.

"You know, Balkis," I say, "I'm not that easy."

"What's that supposed to mean?"

"It means I get that we're after the same thing now,

albeit for different reasons. You want that dress so you can communicate with Lincoln's ghost or some such nonsense. Plus you want it for fortune and glory. I want to uncover it so that it can be proudly displayed in its rightful place. The Smithsonian. Or something like it. You see, Balkis, that dress isn't yours or mine or even the Girvins, be they dead or alive. It belongs to the people of the United States of America and for which it stands and all that jazz."

"Oh, I agree," he says, placing his right hand over his heart like he's about to recite the Pledge of Allegiance. But his act is a lie, and he knows that I know it. "I just want to see the dress finally revealed after all these years."

"Good," I say. "Because otherwise, I'm gonna have to tie you up and leave you here until this thing is finished."

"Please don't even think that way, Mr. Baker. You need me to assist you in the delicate task of exhuming Henry Junior, which I assume must be accomplished illegally. At the very least, you need a second set of eyes. Don't you agree?"

Mofo's got a point. I'll give him that. When Detective Miller handed me this job of finding the Girvins, he more than likely did not expect me to start looking for the dress instead, not to mention engage in something super illegal like grave robbing. But then, he didn't exactly warn me against it either.

"Okay," I say. "But how do I know I can trust you? You've already knocked me over the head once, and tried to blow me up. Then there's the matter of the missing Girvins."

He grows a grin. It tells me he's already thought up a witty retort.

"Well, the bomb was a fake, and you have also

knocked me out. Or knocked Booth out, anyway. We're even. And as for the Girvins, I already told you, I had nothing to do with their slipping off the radar."

Stealing a moment to think.

"Tell you what," I say. "Give me your phone."

His eyes open wide. "Why?"

"Give me your phone and your wallet while you're at it."

"And what, pray tell, difference does it make if I hand over these things to you?"

"Insurance," I say. "Simple as that. You try anything with me and I'll make sure your personals get deep-sixed somewhere where you can't get them back. Like Detective Miller's inbox for instance."

He laughs.

"Not for nothing, Mr. Baker," he says. "But you're unarmed and I'm quite a bit bigger than you."

My open-handed jab connects with his sternum a split second before he realizes I've even thrown a punch. He goes down hard, desperately trying to replace the air I've just knocked out of him.

Down on bended knee, I proceed to empty his pockets of his wallet, phone, and even a nice tight little bundle of cash.

"You're wrong, Balkis," I say. "You're not bigger than me. You're just fatter. And slower. And about as physical as a stick of butter."

He tries to nod while the soft skin on his face turns fifty shades of red.

"Now, you can help me dig up the dress. But if it is, in fact, inside Henry's grave or one of the empty ones beside him like I think it is, it goes to a museum immediately. Agreed?"

"Agreed," he mumbles.

If I weren't about to pull off an illegal exhumation, I

might get on the horn with Miller, let him know that the real story behind Clara Harris/Henry Rathbone doesn't even come close to matching the historical record. Maybe the murder/suicide aspect, but that's about the extent of it. But of course, he'd scream at me for not being on the trail of the missing Girvins.

As I exit the bedroom and start back down the stairs, I picture old lady and old man Girvin, the blood trail they left behind, and the Derringer that had been freshly fired. For now, Balkis and I have to work together to solve this thing. No choice but to swallow my suspicions about his having had everything to do with the old couple's disappearance. Everything to do with their murder.

20

THE DRIVE TO THE ALBANY RURAL CEMETERY TAKES ONLY three minutes at most. What won't take only three minutes is locating the Rathbone plots. But then, if the cemetery visitor center is still open, we might be able to scarf a registry documenting the one hundred seventy years' worth of men, women, and children who've been buried here, including my dad.

Turning into the main entry gates, I follow the winding, tree-lined road into the heart of the old, historic cemetery and take it downhill to the single-story, chapel-like, stone building that serves as its visitor's center. Parking the truck out front, Balkis and I then enter the building through a front, solid wood, six-paneled door that must be at least a century old.

Inside the cavernous vestibule, I spot a bulletin board that's tacked with several announcements, including one for a Civil War reenactment which is to take place on the lower, undeveloped grounds of the cemetery property tomorrow morning. Another announcement asks visitors to keep the grounds clean and to carry out what you haul in, that is, if your idea of a good time is to enjoy a picnic lunch on top of dead people.

"You supposed to be doing battle tomorrow, Mr. Civil War Reenactment Aficionado?"

Balkis turns a shade of pale. "I am indeed expected to participate in the morning. However, my significant other is also expected to be there. Rather, ex-significant other who fights for the Union Army. It could all get a little messy."

"Cavorting with the enemy, Balkis," I say. "Tsk tsk."

"Let's just say I fell in love with someone I shouldn't have."

"The jilted Confederate lover and the Union Yankee meet on the field of battle. Could there be anything worse? You'd better watch your back."

Below the bulletin board is a stack of papers, each one offers a brief history of the old cemetery as well as a listing of nearly all the names belonging to the dead people who occupy each of its plots.

"Bingo," Balkis says, grabbing the sheet. He pats the pockets on his trousers and his vest. "I don't have my reading specs," he adds.

I take the paper from him and begin searching through the list of names until I come to the name *Rathbone.*

"Henry Riggs Rathbone," I say. "Plot number ninety-six. Dad's plot was number three thousand and six, which tells me the Rathbone plots must be located in the older part of the cemetery."

A man enters the vestibule through an interior wood

door. He's a small, mostly bald, old man who looks like he was employed by the cemetery back when it opened in 1841. Smoothing out the jacket on his black suit and straightening his bow tie, he gazes upon Balkis with wide eyes.

"Excuse me, sir," he says, his voice mild mannered and high pitched. "But the Civil War reenactment isn't until tomorrow."

Balkis stands tall, sucking in his beer gut.

"I am not reenacting anything presently, my good sir," he says. "This is my wardrobe of choice."

"My name is Christopher Kendris," the old man states. "I am the cemetery historian." Then, giving Balkis a look, like he's met him before, and perhaps he has, considering the professor's employment at the university and his participation in the war reenactments. "Pardon me for saying so, sir. But you look like John Wilkes Booth...With a couple of extra pounds around the gut."

Balkis sneers. Before he backhands the little guy, I step in between them. Okay, maybe they don't know one another.

"Excuse me," I say. "But my friend here and I are researching a new movie I'm producing on the Civil War and some of its stranger tales. One subject we're working on now is Clara Harris and the dress she wore inside the Presidential Box when Lincoln was shot by Mr. Booth."

Balkis clears his throat as if still trying to pass himself off as the infamous Southern actor.

I add, "This man will be playing the role of Booth in the movie."

Kendris takes on an expression of relief.

"That makes sense," he says. "Lots of movies have been filmed on the cemetery grounds over the years.

Especially period pieces having to do with Civil War era events, or even the Civil war itself." He sighs. "Many fallen Union soldiers are buried up on that hill, you know."

Balkis clears his throat again like the only good Union soldier is a dead Union soldier. That's when I step on his foot, pressing down on his toes with my steel-toed, lace-up, Chippewas utility boots.

"I am aware of that, Mr. Kendris," I say. "We're interested in one family plot in particular. The Rathbones."

"As in Clara and Henry," he says. "Buried up in the old section, their graves are more or less forgotten. I can take you there if you like."

"We'd like," I say.

"I'll grab the keys to my vehicle and meet you outside," Kendris says, entering back through the wood door to some unknown office or mausoleum.

I turn back to Balkis.

"Hell are you doing, whacko?"

"Whatever do you mean?"

"The John Wilkes Booth act. Stop it already. It's weird and could get us in a lot of trouble. This is Yankee country after all."

He smirks. "I'm proud of my southern heritage and Mr. Booth was a patriot who died on behalf of his beliefs."

"So did Hitler. And what do you mean proud of your southern heritage? You're clearly a northerner."

His eyes go wide. "I am trans-geographic. I am a Southerner trapped in a Northerner's body. You would learn to respect my own particular brand of individuality if only you spent a little time on my university campus. Now can you please get off of my foot, Baker?"

I remove my boot. Trans-gender, trans-race, and now trans-geographic. Holy Christ, the entire world has taken a turn for the pathological.

Just then, a car horn honks.

"Follow me and keep quiet," I say.

Together, we exit the visitor's center through the big wood, church-like door.

As promised, the old man has arrived with his car. A Model T Ford that must be closing in on a century. Painted in white block letters on the black door panel are the words, Albany Rural Cemetery, Est. April 2, 1841. Taken together with Girvin's old house, its basement crypt containing the bodies of Clara and Henry Rathbone, plus Balkis acting out his John Wilkes Booth fantasy, and an elusive dress that not only contains the precious blood of Lincoln but that's also said to be cursed—and all sorts of truths turning out to be false and fictions turning out to be true—I'm convinced I've fallen down the rabbit hole.

"What a sharp looking vehicle," Balkis says, clearly excited about the idea of riding in a piece of ancient history.

"Get a hold of yourself, Professor," I whisper under my breath.

We stuff ourselves into the back of the old car.

"Hold on tight," old man Kendris says before grinding the floor-mounted gear shift into first and giving the Model T the gas.

21

WE NEGOTIATE A MAZE OF NARROW GRAVEL ROADS LINED
on both sides with the oldest plots in the cemetery.
Some of the graves have been forgotten and are now
overgrown with grass and weeds, their once white
marble headstones now streaked with gray-black grime
and leaning precariously to one side, as if about to drop
as dead as the men and women they memorialize. Some
of the sites support mausoleums that likely cost more
than my first house. Big stone and marble cathedral-like
monstrosities outfitted with stained glass and mini
chapels meant to honor entire families long since dead
and forgotten by history.

Kendris pulls up to one such grave site which is also
overgrown, its three headstones surrounded by an
undersized black wrought iron fence that's decayed over
the decades since it was constructed. He stares out the

passenger side window and points with extended arm and index finger.

"That one there," he says. "On the far right. That's Henry Junior's. The others belong to Henry and Clara respectively, his parents. The other kids are buried in Germany, or so history tells us."

Don't believe your history...Not in this case...

Balkis and I exchange glances. For a change, we're on the same page. We could say something about the true resting place of Henry and Clara but that would cause a fuss and mess up our plans for recovering the Lincoln dress.

We exit the Model T.

"Thanks," I say to the old man. "We can take it from here."

"Sure you boys don't want me to stick around and give you a little more history of the place for your movie?"

"We're fine on our own," I say. "I know where to find you when we need you."

"Alrighty then," he says, throwing the tranny back into gear. "Have fun with the Rathbones."

He offers a salute and takes off back down the road.

Balkis and I take a moment to gaze upon the old plots. Or maybe I should say, the plots take a moment to gaze upon us. At least, standing there alone in the old overgrown portion of the cemetery, it feels as though a dozen sets of eyes are gazing at us. I'm not one for believing in ghosts, but if I did believe in them, I'd say this place was full of them. My dad's included.

"Something just dawned on me, Baker," Balkis says.

"What is it?"

"What if Henry Junior's coffin is as empty as Clara

and Henry Senior's most certainly are?"

If I were plugged into an electrical outlet, a lightbulb would have just lit up over my head.

"That's the smartest thing you've said all day, Professor."

"It is?"

I step up to the gate of the old iron fence, push it open. Its rusted hinges cry out in pain. Crossing through the tall grass to Clara's awkwardly leaning headstone, I read her short inscription.

Here lie the remains of Clara Harris Rathbone.
Witness to President Lincoln's Assassination.
September 4, 1834 - December 23, 1893

I glance at Henry's false grave, his death date also listed as December 23. Then I take a look at the son, Henry Junior's, grave. His marker inscription lists him as deceased in March of 1946.

"You see, Balkis, I can bet dollars to donuts that after he found his parents bodies down inside that sub-cellar in 1893, young Henry Junior didn't dare touch the bodies because, like I already said, that would be like disturbing the ghost of Lincoln himself or at the very least, disturbing the curse. Instead, he buried the source of the haunting. The source of the curse."

"The dress," Balkis says. "He buried the dress in Clara's grave. After all, it's her dress. And had he held onto it until his own death, he would have been incapable of burying it inside his own casket."

"That's right. The dead aren't capable of accomplishing a whole lot after they're dead." I turn back to him while glancing at my watch. "It's nearly sundown. We wait until full dark. Then, we borrow the cemetery backhoe and solve this puzzle once and for all."

22

By the time we walk back to the truck parked outside the visitor's center, it's already dark. The maintenance shed is located not far from the center, so I simply make the short drive to the brick building and park around back.

Time check.

8:32 PM on a warm summer night.

"We need to wait a while, Balkis," I say. "This operation needs to be conducted not only under the cover of darkness but late night when all the nosy busybodies are fast asleep. Capice?"

"Si, senior," he says, his tone sarcastic. "So, what shall we do in the meantime? Chat it up?"

"Gonna be a long night," I say. "I suggest you get some sleep while you can."

I rest the back of my head against the seat back,

close my eyes. I listen for the sound of Balkis doing the same thing, which he does. Maybe a minute goes by before I begin to hear the familiar sound of snoring.

"That didn't take long," I whisper, knowing full well that I'm not about to sleep a wink with that rattle coming from his overworked lungs.

Three hours later, I'm still awake but somewhat rested. Reaching out, I poke Balkis in the ribs.

"Time to go to work, Professor," I say.

Startled, he wakes wide-eyed.

"Told you I wouldn't be able to sleep," he says.

"Oh, yeah," I say fighting the urge to roll my eyes. "You must be exhausted."

Exiting the truck we walk around to the front of the building and try the door set beside a big, metal, roll-up door. Naturally, it's locked.

"Serious adventure man like you won't let a locked door get in his way," Balkis says, as though issuing me a challenge.

Glancing upwards, I make a quick check for security cameras. None to be seen with the naked eye anyway. But then, judging by the cemetery's seeming commitment to the old and antiquated, I can bet they haven't yet entered the modern era of digitally enhanced security systems.

Reaching into the pocket on my bush jacket, I once more pull out my Swiss Army knife. Opening the big blade, I slip it between the closer and the hollow metal frame and jimmy the door open. Chase the highly skilled.

We both step inside, closing the door behind us.

"Lights," I say.

Balkis feels along the wall, flips a switch which powers up the overheads.

And that's when I see him.
My dead dad.

23

DAD'S OLD, WATER DAMAGED, MOONLIGHT FUNERAL
Home casket is leaning up against the far wall of the
maintenance shed, its cover wide open, his blue-suited
mummified remains standing upright, hands crossed at
the midsection, face black and tight. His eyes, although
sewn shut, somehow stare at me like he's just caught me
coming home far too late from a night partying with my
high school pals.

I stand there, heart in my throat.

"Professor Balkis," I say, "I'd like to introduce you to
my dad."

"Excuse me?" he says, his face having turned
somewhat pale at the sight of Dad's remains.

"The whole reason I'm in town in the first place,
Professor, is to rebury my old man. I guess the workers
didn't have time to rebury him yet, so they stored him in
here."

"What for, Baker?"

"The cemetery calls it a reallocation of space. But from what I'm hearing, the town is taking over a portion of their property for a new access road. In any case, here Dad rests until Albany Rural can find a new piece of ground for him on the cemetery hill."

Balkis swallows. "Why do you think they left the casket lid open like that?"

"Water leaked into the concrete vault. The hinges and latch were rusted out. That casket lid no longer stays shut. He's gonna need a new casket, which is gonna cost me."

Let's hope Miller's word is good regarding that three hundred per day payout for my services...Course, it would help if I started looking for the Girvins instead of spending my time going after a relic of the Lincoln assassination. But then, how can I resist?

"Gee, Baker, your dad looks really dead."

"No more or less dead than Clara and Henry Senior."

"Yeah, but they are all bones. This is different. It's like he's dead, but alive, too, you know. Creepy."

"I thought Southern gentlemen don't use the word 'creepy.'"

"Forgot myself for a moment."

"You sure are an odd duck, you know that, Professor?"

"You think I'm odd," he says. "Wait till you meet the Girvins."

"That is, they're still alive."

He exhales, clearly annoyed.

"Must I repeat myself yet again, Baker? I did not kill the Girvins. They disappeared on their own. End of story."

Me, looking at my watch.

95

"Time's wasting, Professor. We've got work to do."

To the immediate right of Dad sits the backhoe I used this morning to dig him back up. It occurs to me that I'll need an ignition key. To Dad's left is a metal desk covered in paperwork. Mounted to the wall above it is a large map of the entirety of the Albany Rural Cemetery, and mounted beside it is a bulletin board that contains multiple sets of keys hanging from metal hooks.

Making my way to the board, I stand by the desk and examine the keys. I recognize the keys to the Cat backhoe right away since Dad owned one just like it. In fact, I learned the art of sandhogging on that model backhoe, my dad standing over my shoulder, the ever conscientious teacher. I steal them from the hook on the board. Then, opening the desk drawers I search around for something else we're going to need. A flashlight.

I find one in the bottom, right-hand drawer.

Turning, I toss it to the Professor who fumbles the catch but manages to hang on.

"Was never one for sports," he mumbles. "Intellectual pursuits are my game."

"You don't say."

In the far corner of the room are a spade and a crowbar. I grab both and take them with me to the backhoe. Climbing into the cockpit, I insert the key and fire her up. The entire open room explodes with the roar from the old engine.

"The door please, Professor!" I bark over the engine noise.

He turns to eye the two large buttons mounted to the wall beside the entry door and the roll up door. One green button and one red. He chooses green. Thumbing the controls, the ceiling-mounted motor grumbles to life as the heavy duty chain begins to lift the large metal door. When it's fully opened, I shift the backhoe into gear and drive it out of the garage.

Depressing the brake, I call out for the Professor.

"You coming?"

Smoothing out his thick John Wilkes Booth mustache, he offers a nervous nod.

"Naturally I want to be there for the resurrection of the Lincoln dress."

I bet you do...Problem is, what happens if it is indeed buried where I think it's buried? What have you got up your sleeve, Professor?

"Wait," I say. "Shut the light off and close the door. We're taking a chance as it is."

He does it. Kills the light and depresses the red button, lowering the door. Stepping over to the vehicle, he hops onto the runner, steadying himself by gripping the cockpit door.

"Hold tight," I say.

"Wouldn't have it any other way, Baker."

24

I CAN PRACTICALLY HEAR BALKIS' OVER-STRESSED TICKER pounding all the way up the hill to the old part of the cemetery where Clara's tomb is located. I can't decide if he's afraid of getting caught robbing a grave or afraid of getting caught *and* being pinned with the murder of Mr. and Mrs. Girvin. But I can't be concerned with that right now. Right now, I want to find that dress and get it safely away from this place. When that's done, I can call Miller back in and let him in on the truth about the Girvins: that I'm no closer to finding out where they disappeared to now than I was yesterday afternoon. I owe him that much. In the meantime, if Balkis tries anything once the dress is revealed, I'll be ready for him.

When we come upon the old Rathbone plots, I stop the backhoe and Balkis hops off.

"Stand aside," I warn, turning the machine around and backing it into place, the big back wheels pressed up against the short wrought iron fence.

Balkis shifts himself over.

"Flashlight," I say. "Point it at Clara's plot. The headlamps on this backhoe aren't very bright."

He does as instructed, the overgrown green grass now illuminated by the white flashlight and the headlamps. Placing my naked hands on the controls, I feel the heat and the vibration from the idling engine. In my head, I see my dad, hear his voice.

"Gently touch the controls with your fingertips, kid. Don't force them. Let the machine do the work. You just be the brains."

I finger the first lever. The thick, black, hydraulic hoses fill like blood to the vein, and the bucket comes alive extending out and away from the machine like a mechanical arm. Aiming the bucket teeth for what would be considered the head of the plot, or about a foot inwards from where the headstone is planted (anything closer and the already unsteady piece of marble will come crashing down), I plunge the bucket into the grass and cut down through the earth, scooping up my first full load of soil. Touching the other levers as if they were toggles on a video game controller, I dump the load of earth to the side and continue on with the dig.

With Balkis holding the flashlight on the ever expanding rectangular plot, I keep digging until I hit something other than soft earth.

A casket.

That's when I exit the cockpit, grab the chains hanging off the side of the machine.

"Jump down into that hole, Professor," I say, setting one end of the chain onto the backhoe bucket, and the opposite four ends onto the grass beside the open grave.

"Me?" he says, startled.

"One of us has to operate the machine and it sure as hell can't be you."

"What exactly do you want me to do?"

"Hook the ends of the chains onto the casket corners so that we can pull her up."

"What if there's nothing to hang the hooks on?"

"Legitimate question," I say. "Then that means we work together down in that hole to open the casket up."

"Can't we just do that now?"

"Not if we can bring her up. It'll be easier and neater opening her up this way. Now go."

Tentatively, he approaches the open plot. Then, sitting himself down on the edge of the grave, he slides off and drops himself down inside. I estimate Balkis to be about five feet ten or eleven inches, which means his head and shoulders rise above the grass line.

Flashing the light onto the casket, he says, "There're some metal ringlets mounted to each corner of the casket."

"That's what we're looking for," I say. Then, "How's the general condition of the box? You think it will come up without crumbling all to hell?"

He stomps his foot on top of the lid, then jumps up and down.

"Seems pretty solid to me," he says.

"Lucks on our side. Box must be lined with metal. Something that was new for the time. There was probably a glass sealer too, which might still be intact. Also, there's not a body inside it to rot the wood from the inside out. No worm food."

"I get it," he says.

"Attach the chains and let's do this, Professor."

He attaches the hooked ends of the four chains to the black metal ringlets. Then, he lifts himself out of the grave, his genuine 1865 John Wilkes Booth outfit now covered in dirt, mud, and grass stains.

Slipping back into the cockpit, I sit myself down and set my hands on the controls. The bucket begins to slowly raise while the four ends of chain go taught. After a second or two, the bucket and its arm begin to strain as the metal and wood casket is lifted from its resting place for the first time since it was laid in the ground well over a century ago.

Slowly, the dark brown, almost black, casket is revealed as I shift the bucket so that the rectangular box can be set down on the grass. When the job is done, I take hold of the crowbar and jump off the machine.

"I need more of that flashlight, Professor."

He follows me to the casket, flashlight in hand, the white light bouncing off the mud-covered box. Initially, I inspect the closer, which has rusted over the years. I then check the hinges which, too, are rusted.

"Well, here goes nothing and everything," I say, sticking the crowbar into the thin linear space between the lid and the box. I press down on the metal bar with all my strength.

It takes maybe three shoves against the bar before the dark cemetery fills with the sound of a pop and the lid releases.

I take a step back.

"Care to do the honors, Professor?"

That's when I feel the metal gun barrel pressed against the back of my head.

"Whaddaya say we do the honors, bitch," comes the voice of an old man.

25

I SHOOT THE PROFESSOR A LOOK, HIS BIG TREMBLING BODY now lit up in the backhoe headlamps.

"Don't look at me," he says. "I had nothing to do with them following us here."

I'm not sure if I should believe him, or if it even matters at this point.

Looks like I won't have to apologize to Miller after all...

"Down on your fuckin' knees, jerkoff," insists the man I take for old man Girvin.

He and his wife step in between myself and the casket. They might be as old as the hills, but their movements are that of much younger people. Spry and athletic. The old man's got a filthy mouth. And what's this nonsense about his wife and Alzheimer's?

"How long you been watching us?" I ask, lowering myself to my knees.

"Since you broke into my goddamned house yesterday morning," Girvin says. "Ain't that right, Mother?"

She nods. Then, pointing her own pistol at Balkis.

"You too, fatso," she says. "Down on your knees, where you spend most of your time anyway." She laughs at her own quip.

"Betty," the professor pleads. "After all we've been through together. You can't make me succumb to such a heinous idea. Betty and Bill, what's happened to your humanity for God's sakes?"

She raises up the old Colt six shooter, fires off a round that practically singes Balkis' hair. He shrieks and drops down to his knees, dead weight.

Balkis was right about one thing. The Girvins are into their weapons.

"Any more questions, Liberace?" she says.

Me...holding back a chuckle.

In the light of the backhoe headlamps, I can see that Betty, or Mrs. Girvin, is dressed in a wide, brown skirt that must have a hoop under it. Her black shirt is long-sleeved, fits tight to her torso while her white hair is pulled back and held in place with a thick leather barrette. Old Man Bill Girvin is dressed in the blue uniform of the Union Civil War Officer. Judging by his mostly bald scalp, thin, almost fragile limbs, and sunken face, he looks old enough to have served in the uniform back in the day. But with his own Colt six-shooter in hand, he more than makes up for age and frailty.

"Mother," he says, his bloodshot eyes going from me to Balkis to me again, "you've waited long enough. Open the box and see if the dress truly does reside inside the casket."

"So how'd you get away with this, Girvin?" I say, my hands locked together at the fingers, palms pressed flat on top of my head. "You fake your own disappearance and even spice it up by leaving behind a Derringer just like the one Booth shot Lincoln with? You draw a little blood, leave enough behind to make the scene look believable? Taken altogether, all evidence would point to Professor Balkis, who I must admit is a bit of a nut case, as the number one suspect."

"You got a big fat smart mouth for a whippersnapper," Girvin says.

"Whippersnapper," I say. "Now there's an old one you don't hear very often anymore." Then, "How long you been looking for the dress?"

"Depends on how you define looking? That dress is cursed. At first we weren't bothered by it because we didn't really believe in it. But that doesn't mean we were about to test the theory out by disturbing it. Maybe we're crazy, but not *that* bat crazy. As the years went on, we began to take notice of strange things happening. We'd hear voices, screams, things falling off the shelves. Once, back in the fall of '72 or '73, Mother was woken up in the morning by the sound of a woman calling out her name. She went to the window, climbed out of it, and dropped down to the front lawn, breaking her leg. That's when we knew the curse was real and that the dress had to exist somewhere inside the house or close by.

"When we heard through the grapevine that you was coming to rebury your father, we knew we had to somehow get you to the house. Balkis' job was to convince Detective Miller to bring you in. Man of your expertise would be able to sniff out Clara's dress if it existed. Turns out, you were able to sniff out a lot more. You know what, Mr. Baker? We lived in that house nearly seventy years and had no idea Clara and Henry were still living in that second basement...So to speak."

"So to speak," I say. "So when the police asked me to

assist in looking for you two, you knew that I would turn my attention to the Lincoln Dress."

"From what I hear, you can't resist two things: fresh pussy and a treasure hunt."

"Father!" Betty barks.

"Sorry, Mother," he says, nodding her way. Then, eyes back on me. "Mother don't like it when I use the P word."

"Call me an antiquities slut," I say, "but I should have seen through your charade a lot sooner than this. I must be losing my edge. But answer me this? Why not cut through the floor and break through the brick wall yourself? You might have ended this mystery decades ago."

"Not on your life," old lady Girvin chimes in. "Only reason I agreed to this here little operation is because Father and I are getting on in years and might not have us another shot. What you must keep in mind, Mr. Baker, is this: He who finds the dress will be recipient of a curse so awful his skin will eventually melt off his bones and he will never know a good night's sleep again because the ghosts of Abe Lincoln, John Wilkes Booth, Clara Harris, and Henry Rathbone will be shouting in your ears."

"Jeeze," I say. "Will I have chronic bad gas, too?"

"Hey look on the bright side, Baker," Bill Girvin says. "Looks to me like you've finally located the dress. Seems like you still got it even if the job ain't gonna get you laid. 'Less, of course, you think Balkis here is cute. And don't you worry none about that God awful curse, 'cause we're gonna have to bury you and Balkis along with Clara's empty coffin when this thing is done." The old man glances over his shoulder. "How you doing, Mother?"

Locking eyes on her, I watch her lift the casket lid

just a few inches. But, just like Dad's casket, the hinges are so rusted, they snap in two under the weight of the metal and wood lid, and it drops down into the open grave. She turns back to her husband.

"There's a box," she says. "A metal strongbox. It's locked with a padlock."

"Don't you go near it!" he shouts. "You let the boys here do the dangerous work."

Girvin is torn between paying attention to her and then to me and Balkis. Also, the arm that supports the pistol seems to be getting tired. That's when I slowly shift my gaze to Balkis.

"On...my...count," I mouth.

His eyes light up like a high wattage bulb. He might be a trans-geographic whacko, but he understands perfectly well what I've got cooked up in my head.

"One...two...three..."

I lunge for the old man, wrapping my arms around his legs like I'm taking down an injury-plagued, way-beyond-his-prime quarterback.

Balkis goes after Betty, thrusting his bulbous head into her stomach.

"That's for making fun of me!" he shouts.

She drops the pistol, goes down hard on her back. But the old man has, by some miracle, still managed to hold onto his. He's trying to aim it at my head so that he can make jelly filling out of my brains.

I grip his shooting wrist and jam my thumb in the sensitive space between his arm and wrist. The pistol drops and he releases a scream that sounds like a rabid dog that's been run over by a stagecoach.

"You wouldn't dare harm a frail old man," he says from down on his knees.

"I wouldn't dream of it, bitch."

Making a tight fist, I bury it in his face.

106

26

TEN MINUTES LATER, THE GIRVIN THREAT HAS BEEN officially neutralized now that Balkis and I have hogtied the two of them with black electrical tape from a roll we found in the backhoe cockpit. Off on the eastern horizon, over the blue mountains of Massachusetts, the dawn is breaking.

"We don't have much time," Balkis says. "The maintenance crew will be back soon."

I glance at my watch. Six fifteen in the morning. Time flies when your life is on the line. Coming from out of the distance, the crack of gunfire. Then a series of thunderous booms that resonates across the valley and that can only come from cannon fire. It's all followed by screams and a collective roar of voices.

"That's the Rebel yell," Balkis says, his eyes aglow like he's been touched by an angel. "They've started without me."

Pulse picks up. "They've begun their reenactment down in the valley. It must begin at dawn. Just like the real thing."

"Yes," Balkis slowly nods. "A dawn charge. Oh, how I wish I were with my boys." Then, "Let's open that box, Baker."

"Roger that," I say. "And get this place cleaned up."

The crowbar back in hand, I approach the open casket and take a knee. The strongbox is made of metal and the padlock that secures it looks formidable enough. But what I'm banking on is that the non-alloy metal has weakened over the decades, making it possible for me to snap the clasp in two. Shoving the straight end of the bar into the U-shaped clasp, I grip the bar with both hands and heave upwards.

The clasp snaps in two like a stale pretzel.

Removing the padlock, I then place my hands on the strongbox cover. With Balkis watching wide-eyed over my shoulder, I open it. What we both discover steals our breath away.

27

THEY'RE NEATLY PLACED ON TOP OF THE DRESS. THE TRUE
Derringer and fighting knife that were used to kill
Lincoln and wound Major Rathbone. As for the dress
itself, it's tightly folded like a funeral flag, like it was
placed inside the box only yesterday by Clara Harris's
son. The blood stains have darkened over the years.
They appear almost black, rather than red or auburn.
The cloth is a fine smooth linen with satin frills that are
visible even in its folded state.

Balkis reaches in. But I grab hold of his hand.

"Not now," I say. "Bad enough we've exposed these
relics to the air. But to unfold that dress out here in the
elements will immediately begin the process of its rapid
disintegration. These artifacts need to be examined in a
laboratory."

I release his hand and he pulls it back.

Closing the box, I lift it out of the casket and set it aside. Pressing both hands against the casket, shove it into the open grave. That's also when Balkis presses his hands against my back and pushes me into the hole along with it.

28

THE BACK OF MY HEAD BOUNCES OFF THE OLD COFFIN, knocking me silly for maybe a full minute before I realize what's happened. Another round of cannon fire reverberates throughout the cemetery followed by a cavalcade of small arms fire. More screams follow that. I also make out the sound of the backhoe engine. My blurred vision focuses on something hovering over the open grave.

It's the backhoe bucket.

The bucket swings downwards fast, and a pile of dirt and mud splash down over me, covering my face and body. I breathe in and choke on the dirt. Balkis is attempting to bury me alive so he can get rid of my body of evidence along with Clara's empty casket. Then, he can keep the Lincoln dress for himself. Why the hell didn't I see this coming earlier? How stupid of me to assume Balkis didn't know how to operate a backhoe? What a fucking rookie mistake turning my back on him in the first place.

I roll over, try and steal a breath of fresh air. Try and pick myself up. But my head is still ringing and I'm too weak to lift the weight of my upper body. I hear, and feel, the presence of the backhoe bucket only a few feet overhead. Another load of dirt falls onto my back. The weight of the earth causes me to drop onto the casket. For a second or two, I just lie there, knowing that if I don't work up the strength necessary to pull myself out of this hole, I'm already a dead man.

But I'm so exhausted, so dizzy, that I want to lie still, allow the dirt to bury my body. Maybe I was destined to become a permanent part of this excavation. The true occupant of Clara Harris's grave.

But I can't give up. Can't allow that to happen. Can't allow Balkis to get away with the dress. Get away with murder.

In my spinning brain, I see my dad. See him inside that open casket laid up against the wall in the maintenance shed. I see him come alive, his sewn together eyelids opening, his face regaining its original shape and color. His mouth opening.

"Come on, Chase!" he shouts. *"Get the hell up. Get yourself out of that hole and put this thing right."*

The bucket is raised over the hole once more. It's about to drop and dump a third load onto my head. A third load which is sure to finish me off. Pulling myself up through the weight of that much dirt will be impossible.

"Come on, Chase!" Dad insists. *"Save yourself already!"*

Sucking in one last breath, I assume push-up position and lift, breaking myself out of the dirt.

Bounding up onto my knees and then my feet, I reach up, plant my hands on the ground and heave my body out of the grave.

I shoot a glance up at the backhoe cockpit, see Balkis' eyes go wide as if he fully expects me to be dead already. Dead and buried.

He shifts the bucket over my prone body. The bucket falls. But at the last split second, I roll out from under it, the heavy steel weight pounding the earth beneath me.

More cannon fire erupts from down in the valley.

I jump up to my feet, run to the backhoe. But Balkis has already lifted himself out of the seat. He jumps off the backhoe and begins sprinting downhill in the direction of the battle reenactment.

True to my name, I make chase.

29

HE'S FASTER THAN A MAN OF THAT WEIGHT AND PHYSICAL
condition should be. Or maybe I'm still suffering from
the effects of being buried alive. As we run, the sounds
of war fill the senses. Rifles firing. Cannon rounds
exploding. Sabers rattling. Men screaming as though
their legs and arms are being blasted off for real.

After a few seconds, I can make out the battlefield
that occupies the acres of unutilized Albany Rural
Cemetery green field. A flat plain that exists at the
bottom of the cemetery hill that's now filled with a blue
army colliding with a ragtag army dressed all in gray
and black—the former holding up the Union Stars and
Stripes, the latter waving the Stainless Banner of the
Confederate States of America. The morning air is thick
with black and white smoke from the cannon and
musket fire, the earth no doubt trembling beneath the
reenactment soldier's booted feet.

As I gain ground on Balkis, I'm not thinking about apprehending him in order to hand him over to Detective Miller. I'm thinking about how absurd it is to find enjoyment in replaying a battle in which hundreds or thousands of young men were either killed outright or horribly wounded.

"Balkis!" I shout after a time. "You can't escape!"

He turns.

"That dress is mine!" he shouts. "Lincoln crowned himself the king of America and he made the Union the tool to wipe out slavery. The blood of the tyrant is on my hands and my hands only. *Sic Semper Tyrannis*...Thus always to tyrants."

Oh, Christ, John Wilkes Booth is back again...

All that shouting has winded him even if we are running downhill. He's only about twenty feet ahead of me when he reaches the bottom and enters into the battle, maybe hoping he can disappear in the smoke and the confusion. But I follow anyway, knowing all it will take is one last sprint on my part and I will be on the son of a bitch like flies on open wounds.

I'm dodging a column of Union soldiers when I catch sight of one soldier who breaks formation, shoulders his musket and, his thickly black-bearded face filled with a smile, plants a bead directly on Balkis.

"Bradly!" Balkis barks. Raising up his hands in surrender, "However in the world can we work this out?"

"We don't, cheater," Bradly says with all the coldness of a corpse, before triggering his weapon.

30

TEN MINUTES LATER I FIND MYSELF SHAKING MY HEAD AT the battlefield scene.

It looks silly, if not absurd.

A fully modern EMT van, its LED flashers lit up, its engine idling, its radio spewing forth tinny messages, parked in the middle of a Civil War-era battlefield. It's like an alien craft has descended upon the place, breaking up the battle for good.

But the ambulance isn't really necessary since the steel ball that entered Balkis' chest and exited his back blew out about a third of his torso, killing him instantly. Making a surreal situation even more bizarre, are the Albany PD cruisers that dot the open field. One of the vehicle's back seats occupied with a handcuffed Union soldier named Bradly who went just a little too far in his zeal to recreate the Civil War battle by loading his rifle with a real musket ball. But then, that's not entirely accurate since the man already confessed to Miller about his long-time affair with Professor Balkis who recently ditched him for a far younger model. What occurred on the battlefield had little to do with zeal, but instead premeditated murder.

Standing there looking into the car at the man's black-bearded face, I'm reminded of my initial thoughts regarding the lunacy of war reenactments. As if the real thing hadn't been looney enough. I'm also reminded that love, no matter what form it takes, can truly stink sometimes.

A tap on the shoulder.

I turn to see the gray-haired Detective Miller standing tall and stone-faced.

"You wanna explain to me the idiocy of all this, Baker?" he says as if truly disturbed at men spending their weekend shooting at one another. Even if the guns were loaded only with blanks. All but one gun that is.

"I was just thinking the same thing, Detective."

He clears his throat. "Ummm, you realize, I could bust you right now for digging up that grave without an authorization."

"Ummm," I mumble, "you didn't tell me not to do it either, Detective."

He smiles, breaking the stone hardness of his face. "Good point. But then, if I fail to tell you not to burn down city hall, will you get the matches out?"

"The dress and the weapons," I say. "They're in a safe place?"

"Presently being delivered to university officials who will place everything under lock and key in the university archeological museum laboratory. They plan on inviting you to the formal unveiling as soon as they can set a date the experts can all agree upon. That is, you're not off gallivanting in some remote corner of the world."

"I don't gallivant, Detective. I explore...You know, like *Dora the Explorer*."

He laughs.

"What about the Girvin's?" I add. "What will happen to them?"

He rolls his eyes.

"Who knows," he says. "They've been delivered to the Albany Medical Center to undergo observations in the wake of their, let's call it, graveside altercation. After that, I'm not sure I have a reason to hold them other than for faking their own disappearance and/or deaths. I suppose I could get them on assault with a deadly weapon. That is, you press charges and send a pair of nutty ninety-year-olds to prison."

Making a smirk, I shake my head. "You're right, they're old and living on another planet. They just wanted to uncover that dress before they died, curses be damned. When they heard I was coming to town, they cooked up the stupid plot along with Balkis to fake their disappearance. That Derringer and the blood was a nice touch because it looked to me like it connected them directly to the Professor. Naturally, I assumed he was the one responsible for their unfortunate demise.

"But when they showed up graveside pointing those old pistols at us, I thought Balkis was off the hook *and* off his rocker. But that was a part of their plan, too. In the end, we all wanted the dress for our own reasons. The Girvins, because they felt they were entitled to it as owner and caretaker of Clara Harris's and Henry Rathbone's Cherry Tree house...Balkis, so that his alter ego, John Wilkes Booth, could somehow own and control the ghost of Abraham Lincoln...and finally, myself, because the Lincoln dress is a part of history, and therefore a part of who we are as free and equal Americans."

"Wow, Baker, that just about brought a tear to my eye," he says. "But the good folks at the Ford's Theater National Historic site have no idea that the Derringer and knife they have hanging on display are as fictional as one of your novels. I'm sure they'll be happy to obtain the real McCoy's along with Clara's dress."

"If I write a book about this adventure, I'll dedicate it to you since I could not have written it without you." Then, "I trust you won't forget my payment."

Out the corner of my eye, part way up the cemetery hill, I spot the old backhoe I used for digging up Clara's grave. There's a flatbed truck parked beside it. The bed contains a casket. My gut tells me that Dad has finally found a new home.

"My heart swells with joy," Miller says sarcastically. "I might even read it. And yeah, just forward your bill to me care of the Albany Police Department, South Pearl Street Division."

The EMT van pulls away, it's siren off, but the flashers shining brightly even on a sun-drenched summer morning.

"Think he knew what hit him?" I say.

"I think Balkis died exactly the way he would have wanted to go. Just like John Wilkes Booth one hundred and fifty years ago when he was slain by a Union soldier's round. Too bad Balkis' bullet had to come from his jilted lover. I guess sometimes truth is far stranger than fiction. You couldn't have written it any better, Baker."

Out the corner of my eye, I catch sight of the abandoned Confederate flag that now sits on the torn-up ground like a discarded dish towel.

"The final shot has officially been fired in the war

between the states. Balkis is the final casualty. May the Union and its free men and women live on forever and ever." My eyes, shifting towards the hill. "If you'll excuse me, Detective, I need to bid a special person a final goodbye."

Reaching into my pockets, I pull out Balkis' phone and his wad of cash.

"The professor's personal effects," I say, handing them over to the detective.

"Keep the cash," he says. "You earned it and from what I'm detecting, you could use it. At the very least, buy yourself a steak dinner."

"No thanks," I say. "It's probably cursed."

I start walking away from the battlefield, towards the cemetery hill.

"I'll be in touch, Baker," Miller says. "There's still the issue of those skeletons down in the Cherry Tree basement."

Glancing at the cop over my shoulder.

"Leave them be," I say. "Close up the opening for good. Fill it in with concrete. Sometimes a skeleton in the closet should remain a skeleton in the closet."

"Maybe you're right, Baker. Maybe, in this case, the right thing to do is to leave history to the worms."

EPILOGUE

THE MAINTENANCE TEAM IS JUST ABOUT READY TO SEAL
Dad's brand new, dark brown, aluminum alloy casket
when I finally make it back up the hill.

"You mind giving me a minute, fellas?" I say as the
two workers back-step away from the flatbed.

"Take all the time you need, Mr. Baker," one of them
says.

I go to the flatbed, disengage the casket lock by
twisting it counter-clockwise, and open the lid. I look
down upon the body for what will certainly be the final
time. I take in the dark blue suit, the faded white shirt,
the neatly tied tie, the dark hands, one placed atop the
other, the skeletal-like face, the sewn shut eyes that no
longer have any shape now that the eyeballs have dried
up, the pinned carnation that still exists after all this
time even if the flower petals have dried and withered to

a brown/black death no different than the man they adorn. A body of the earth about to become a part of the earth once more and forever. A body with its soul long departed, but a body that still belongs to my dad.

"Well, Dad," I say, "I guess this is it. I hope you like your new home. It overlooks the valley, and you'll get the morning sun rising from out of the East. You always liked waking up at dawn before heading off to dig something up. Gave you some peace, I think."

Dad's been gone going on six years now, but I feel my throat closing in on itself and my eyes welling up. I guess I miss the old guy more than I thought. I will keep on missing him too. That's what happens to the ones left behind. That's history's bittersweet gift. No amount of earth or concrete covering or worms can ever take that away.

Reaching out, I straighten the old, dried up carnation as best I can without breaking it. Then, lowering my fingers, I touch Dad's hands once more. They're cold and feel like plastic. Not like when I was a kid and he'd hold my far smaller hand in his while we stood together at the ice cream shop window. Somehow, the touch of his lifeless skin transports me back to a time that was so long ago, but that seems like it transpired in the blink of an eye.

Closing the casket lid, I twist the lock clockwise and seal my father inside for all eternity. Tossing a "thank you" nod to the workers, I wipe my eyes with the back of my hand and head down the cemetery hill, the bright morning sunshine warm on my face.

THE END

If you enjoyed this Chase Baker Thriller, please explore *The Shroud Key* (Chase Baker No.1), *Chase Baker and the Golden Condor* (Chase Baker No. 2), and *Chase Baker and the God Boy* (Chase Baker No. 3)

NOTE: The author has exercised more than a few liberties when it comes to the facts behind the saga of Clara Harris Rathbone and her husband, Henry. For the real story behind their tragic lives and deaths, go to http://blog.nyhistory.org/attending-fords-theater-with-the-lincolns-the-tragic-lives-of-clara-harris-and-henry-rathbone/.

ABOUT THE AUTHOR

Winner of the International Thriller Writer's Paperback Original for 2015, Vincent Zandri is the *New York Times* and *USA Today* bestselling author of more than sixteen novels, including *Everything Burns, The Innocent, The Remains, Orchard Grove,* and *The Shroud Key.* He is also the author of the Shamus Award nominated Dick Moonlight PI series. A freelance photojournalist and solo traveler, he is the founder of the blog *The Vincent Zandri Vox.* He lives in Albany, New York. For more, go to http://www.vincentzandri.com/.